Also by Helen Phillips

The Beautiful Bureaucrat

And Yet They Were Happy

Here Where the Sunbeams Are Green

SOME POSSIBLE SOLUTIONS

SOME POSSIBLE SOLUTIONS

STORIES

HELEN PHILLIPS

HENRY HOLT & COMPANY   NEW YORK

Henry Holt and Company, LLC
Publishers since 1866
175 Fifth Avenue
New York, New York 10010
www.henryholt.com

Henry Holt ® and ® are registered trademarks of Henry Holt and Company, LLC.

Distributed in Canada by Raincoast Book Distribution Limited

Some of these stories have appeared elsewhere, in slightly different form: "The Knowers" in *Electric Literature's Recommended Reading*; "The Messy Joy of the Final Throes of the Dinner Party" on PRI's *Selected Shorts*, commissioned by Symphony Space; "Life Care Center" in *The Iowa Review*, winner of *The Iowa Review* Award; "The Joined" in *Mississippi Review*, finalist for the *Mississippi Review* Prize; "Flesh and Blood" in *Tin House*; "When the Tsunami Came" in *The Pinch*; "One of Us Will Be Happy; It's Just a Matter of Which One" in *Fairy Tale Review*; "Things We Do" in *DIAGRAM*, winner of *DIAGRAM*'s Innovative Fiction Contest; "R" in *Unstuck*; "Children" in *Tin House*; "The Worst" in *ArtFaccia*; "How I Began to Bleed Again After Six Alarming Months Without" in *Unstuck*; "The Beekeeper" in *Isthmus*; and "The Wedding Stairs" in *Slice*.

The italicized quotations in "When the Tsunami Came" are excerpted from the *New York Times* article "For Elderly, Echoes of World War II Horrors" by Martin Fackler (March 14, 2011).

Library of Congress Cataloging-in-Publication Data

Names: Phillips, Helen, 1983– author.
Title: Some possible solutions : stories / Helen Phillips.
Description: New York : Henry Holt and Co., 2016.
Identifiers: LCCN 2015046062 | ISBN 9781627793797 (hardcover) |
ISBN 9781627793803 (ebook)
Subjects: | BISAC: FICTION / Short Stories (single author). | FICTION / Literary.
Classification: LCC PS3616.H45565 A6 2016 | DDC 813/.6—dc23
LC record available at http://lccn.loc.gov/2015046062

Henry Holt books are available for special promotions and premiums.
For details contact: Director, Special Markets.

First Edition 2016

Designed by Meryl Sussman Levavi

ISBN: 978-1-250-13218-5

P1

for Adam

CONTENTS

THE KNOWERS

1.

There are those who wish to know, and there are those who don't wish to know. At first Tem made fun of me in that condescending way of his (a flick of my nipple, a grape tossed at my nose) when I claimed to be among the former; when he realized I meant it, he grew anxious, and when he realized I really did mean it, his anxiety morphed into terror.

"*Why?*" he demanded tearfully in the middle of the night.

I couldn't answer. I had no answer.

"This isn't only about you, you know," he said. "It affects me too. Actually, maybe it affects me more than it affects you. I don't want to sit around for a bunch of decades awaiting the worst day of my life."

Touched, I reached out to squeeze his hand in the dark.

Grudgingly, he squeezed back. I would have preferred to be like Tem, of course I would have! If only I could have known it was possible to know and still accepted ignorance. But now that the technology had been mastered, the knowledge was available to every citizen for a nominal fee.

Tem stood in the doorway as I buttoned the blue wool coat he'd given me for, I think, our four-year anniversary a couple years back.

"I don't want to know where you're going," he said.

"Fine," I said, matter-of-factly checking my purse for my keys, my eyedrops. "I won't tell you."

"I forbid you to leave this apartment," he said.

"Oh hon." I sighed. I did feel bad. "That's just not in your character."

With a tremor, he fell away from the doorway to let me pass. He slouched against the wall, arms crossed, staring at me. His eyes wet and so very dark. Splendid Tem.

After I stepped out, I heard the dead bolt sliding into place.

"So?" Tem said when I unlocked the dead bolt, stepped back inside. He was standing right there in the hallway, his eyes darker than ever, his slouch more pronounced. I was willing to believe he hadn't moved in the 127 minutes I'd been gone.

"So," I replied forcefully. I was shaken, I'll admit it, but I refused to shake him with my shakenness.

"You . . . ?" He mouthed the question more than spoke it.

I nodded curtly. No way was I going to tell him about the bureaucratic office with its pale yellow walls that either smelled like urine or brought that odor to mind. It never ceases to amaze me that, even as our country forges into the future with ever more bedazzling devices and technologies, the archaic infrastructure rots away beneath our feet, the pavement and the rails, the schools and the DMV. In any case: Tem would not know, today or ever, about the place I'd gone, about the humming machine that looked like a low-budget ATM (could they really do no better?), about the chilly metal buttons of the keypad into which I punched my social security number after waiting in line for over forty-five minutes behind other soon-to-be Knowers. There was a silent, grim camaraderie among us; surely I was not the only one who felt it. Yet carefully, deliberately, desperately, I avoided looking at their faces as they stepped away from the machine and exited the room. Grief, relief—I didn't want to know. I had to do what I'd come to do. And what did my face look like, I wonder, as I glanced down at the paper the slot spat out at me, as I folded it up and stepped away from the machine?

Tem held his hand out, his fingers spread wide, his palm quivering but receptive.

"Okay, lay it on me," he said. The words were light, almost jovial, but I could tell they were the five hardest words he'd ever uttered. I swore to never again accuse Tem of being less than courageous. And I applauded myself for going straight from the office to the canal, for standing there above the sickly greenish water, for glancing once more at the piece of paper, for tearing it into as many scraps as possible though it was essentially a scrap to begin with, for dropping it into the factory-scented breeze. I'd thought it was the right thing to do, and now I knew it was. Tem should not have to live under the same roof with that piece of paper.

"I don't have it," I said brightly.

"You don't?" he gasped, suspended between joy and confusion. "You mean you changed your—"

Poor Tem.

"I got it," I said, before he could go too far down that road. "I got it, and then I got rid of it."

He stared at me, waiting.

"I mean, after memorizing it."

I watched him deflate.

"Fuck you," he said. "I'm sorry, but fuck you."

"Yeah," I said sympathetically. "I know."

"You *do* know!" he raged, seizing upon the word. "You *know! You* know!"

He was thrashing about, he was so pissed, he was grabbing me, he was weeping, he half-collapsed upon me. I navigated us down the hallway to the old couch.

When he finally quieted, he was different. Maybe different than he'd ever been.

"Tell me," he calmly commanded. His voice just at the threshold of my hearing.

"Are you sure?" I said. My voice sounded too loud, too hard. In that moment I found myself, my insistence on knowing, profoundly annoying. Suddenly it seemed quite likely that I'd made a catastrophic error. The kind of error that could ruin the rest of my life.

Tem nodded, gazed at me.

I got wildly scared; I who'd so boldly sought knowledge now did not even dare give voice to a date.

Tem nodded again, controlled, miserable. It was my responsibility to inform him.

"April 17—" I began.

But Tem shrieked before I could finish. "Stop!" he cried, shoving his fingers into his ears, his calmness vanished. "Never mind! Don't don't don't!"

"*OKAY!*" I screamed, loud enough that he could hear it through his fingers. It was lonely—ever so lonely—to hold this knowledge alone. April 17, 2043: a tattoo inside my brain. But it was as it should be. It was the choice I had made. Tem wished to be spared, and spare him I would.

2.

It was an okay life span. Not enough—is it ever enough?—but enough to have a life; enough to work a job, to raise children, perhaps to meet a grandchild or two. Certainly abbreviated, though; shorter than average; too short, yes; but not tragically short.

And so in many ways I could live a life like any other. Like Tem's. I could go blithely along, indulging my petty concerns, lacking perspective, frequently forgetting I wasn't immortal. Yet it would be a lie if I said a single day passed without me thinking about April 17, 2043.

In those early years, I'd sink into a black mood come mid-April. I'd lie in bed for a couple of days, clinging to the sheets, my heart a big swollen wound. Tem would bring me cereal, tea. But after the kids were born I had no time for such self-indulgence, and I began to mark the date in smaller, kinder ways. Would buy myself a tiny gift, a bar of dark chocolate or a few daffodils. As time went on, I permitted myself slightly more elaborate gestures—a new dress, an afternoon champagne at some hushed bar. I always felt extravagant on that day; I'd leave a tip of thirty percent, hand out a five-dollar bill to any vagrant who happened to cross my path. *You can't take it with you* and all that.

Tem tried hard to forget what he'd heard, but every time April 17 came around again, I could feel his awareness of it, a slight buzz in the way he looked at me, tenderness and fury rolled up in one. "Oh," he'd say, staring hard at the daffodils as I stepped through the door. *"That."*

I'd make a reservation for us at a fancy restaurant; I'd schedule a weekend getaway. Luxuries we went the whole rest of the year without. Meanwhile, my birthday languished unnoticed in July.

Tem would sigh and pack his overnight case. We sat drinking coffee in rocking chairs on the front porch of a bed-and-breakfast on a hill in the chill of early spring. Tem was generous to me; it was his least favorite day of the year, but he managed to pretend. We'd stroll. We'd eat ice cream. Silly little Band-Aids.

My life would seem normal—bland, really—to an outside observer, but I tell you that for me it has been rich, layered and rich. I realize that it just looks like 2.2 children, an office job and a long marriage, an average number of blessings and curses, but there have been so many moments, almost an infinity of moments—soaping up the kids' hair when they were tiny, walking from the parking lot to the office on a bird-studded Friday morning, smelling the back of Tem's neck in the middle of the night. What can I say. I don't mean to be sentimental, but these are not small things. As the cliché of our time goes, *The deeper that sorrow carves into your being, the more joy you can contain.* This is no time to go into the ups and downs, the stillbirths and the car accident and the estrangement and what happened to my brother, but I will say that I believe the above statement to be true.

April 17. I'd lived that date thirty-one times already before I learned about April 17, 2043. Isn't it macabre to know that we've lived the date of our death many times, passing by it each year as the calendar turns? And doesn't it perhaps deflate that horror just a bit to take the mystery out of it, to actually *know,* to not have every date bear the heavy possibility of someday being the date of one's death?

I do not know the answer to this question.

April 17, 2043. The knowledge heightened my life. The knowledge burdened my life. I regretted knowing. I was grateful to know.

I've never been the type to bungee jump or skydive, yet in many small ways I lived more courageously than others. More courageously than Tem, for instance. I knew when to fear death, yes, but that also meant I knew when not to fear it. I'd gone to the grocery store during times of quarantine. I'd volunteered at the hospital, driven in blizzards, ridden roller coasters so rickety Tem wouldn't let the kids on them.

But December 31, 2042, was a fearful day for me.

"Are you okay?" Tem said after the kids had gone home. We'd hosted everyone for a last supper of the year, both children and their spouses, and our son's six-month-old, our first grandchild, bright as a brand-new penny. At the dinner table, our radiant daughter and her blushing husband announced that they were expecting in August. Amid the raucous cheers and exclamations, no one noticed that I wasn't cheering or exclaiming. The child I'd miss by four months. The ache was vast, vast. I couldn't speak. I watched them, their hugs and high-fives, as though from behind a glass wall.

"Oh god, Ellie," Tem said painfully, sinking onto the couch in the dark living room. "Oh god."

"No," I lied, joining him on the couch. "Not this year."

Tem embraced me so warmly, with such relief, that I felt cruel. I couldn't bear myself. I stood up and, unsteady with dread, limped toward the bathroom.

"Ellie?" he said. "You're limping?"

"My foot fell asleep," I lied again, yanking the door shut behind me.

I stood there in the bathroom, hunched over the sink, clinging to the sink, staring at my face in the mirror until it no longer felt like my face. This would become a distasteful but addictive habit over the course of the next three and a half months.

Aside from the increasing frequency with which I found myself falling into myself in the bathroom mirror, I got pretty good at hiding my dread. From Tem, and even, at times, from myself. We planted bulbs; we bought a cooler for summer picnics. I pretended and pretended; it felt nice to pretend.

Yet when Tem asked, on April 10, what I'd planned for this year's getaway, the veil fell away. Given the circumstance, I had—of course—neglected to make any plans for the seventeenth. Dread rushed outward from my gut until my entire body was hot and cold.

Panicking, I looked across the table at Tem, who was gazing at me openly, boyishly, the way he'd looked at me for almost four decades. Tem and I—we've been so lucky in love.

"Tem," I choked.

"You okay?" he said.

And then he realized.

"Damn it, Ellie!" he yelled and hit the table.

I quietly quit my job, handed in the paperwork, and Tem took the week off, and we spent every minute together. We invited the blissfully ignorant kids out for brunch (I clutched the baby, forced her to stay in my lap even as she tried to wiggle and whine her way out, until eventually I had to hand her over to her mother, a chunk of my heart squirming away from me). Everything I saw—a fire hydrant, a tree, a flagpole—I thought how it would go on existing, just the same. Tem and I had more sex than we'd had in the previous twelve months combined. Briefly I hung suspended and immortal in orgasm, and a few times, lying sun-stroked in bed in the late afternoon, felt infinite. What can I say, what did we do? We held hands under the covers. We made fettuccine Alfredo and, cleaning the kitchen, listened to our favorite broadcast. I dried the dishes with a green dishcloth, warm and damp.

3.

On the morning of April 17, 2043, I was astonished to open my eyes to the light. Six hours and four minutes into the day, and I was alive. Petrified, too scared to move even a muscle, I wondered how death would come for me. I supposed I'd been hoping it would come mercifully, in the soft sleep of early morning. I turned to Tem, who wasn't in bed beside me.

"Tem!" I cried out.

He was in the doorway before I'd reached the "m," his face stricken.

"Tem," I said plaintively, joyously. He looked so good to me, standing there holding two coffee mugs, his ancient baby-blue robe.

"I thought you were dying!" he said.

I thought you were dying. It sounded like a figure of speech. But he meant it so literally, so very literally, that I gave a short sharp laugh.

Would it be a heart attack, a stroke, a tumble down the basement stairs? I had the inclination to stay in bed resting my head on Tem, see if I might somehow sneak through the day, but by 10 a.m. I was still alive and feeling antsy, defiant. Why lie here whimpering when it was coming for me no matter what?

"Let's go out," I said.

Tem looked at me doubtfully.

"It's not like I'm sick or anything." I threw the sheets aside, stood up, pulled on my old comfy jeans.

The outside seemed more dangerous—there it could be a falling branch, a malfunctioning crane, a vehicle running a red light. But it could just as easily catch me at home—misplaced rat poison, a chunk of meat lodged in my throat, a slick bathtub.

"Okay," I said as I stepped out the door, Tem hesitant behind me.

We walked, looking this way and that as we went, hyperaware of everything. Vigilant. I felt like a newborn person, passing so alertly through the world. It was such an anti-death day; the crocuses. Tem kept saying these beautiful, solemn one-liners that would work well if they happened to be the last words he ever said to me, but what I really wanted to hear was throwaway words (all those thousands of times Tem had said "What?" patiently or irritably or absentmindedly), so eventually I had to tell him to please stop.

"You're stressing me out," I said.

"*I'm* stressing *you* out?" Tem scoffed. But he did stop saying the solemn things. We strolled and got coffee, we strolled some more and got lunch, we sat in a park, each additional moment a small shock, we sat in another park, we got more coffee, we strolled and got dinner. Mirrors and windows reminded me that we were a balding shuffling guy hanging on to a grandmother in saggy jeans, but my senses felt bright and young, supremely sensitive to the taste of the coffee, the color of the rising grass, the sound of kids whispering on the playground. I felt carefree and at the same time the opposite of carefree, as though I could sense the seismic activity taking place beneath the bench where we sat, gazing up at kites. Is it strange to say that this day reminded me of the first day I'd ever spent with Tem, thirty-eight years ago?

The afternoon gave way to a serene blue evening, the moon a sharp and perfect half, and we sat on our small front porch, watching cars glide down our street. At times the air buzzed with invisible threat, and at times it just felt like air. But the instant I noticed it just felt like air, it would begin to buzz with invisible threat once more.

Come 11:45 p.m., we were inside, brushing our teeth, shaking. Tem dropped his toothbrush in the toilet. I grabbed it out for him. Would I simply collapse onto the floor, or would it be a burglar with a weapon?

What if there had been an error? Remembering back to that humble machine, that thin scrap of paper, the cold buttons of the keypad, I indulged in the fantasy I'd avoided over the years. It suddenly seemed possible that I'd punched my social in wrong, one digit off. Or that there had been some kind of systemic mistake, some malfunction deep within the machine. Or perhaps I'd mixed up the digits—April 13, 2047. If I lived beyond April 17, 2043, where would the new boundaries of my life lie?

Shakily, I rinsed Tem's toothbrush in steaming hot water from the faucet; it wouldn't be me lingering in the aisle of the drugstore, considering the potential replacements, the colors.

We stood there staring at each other in the bathroom mirror. This time I didn't fall into my own reflection—Tem, I was looking at Tem.

Why had it never occurred to me that it might be something that would kill him too?

In all of these years, truly, I had never once entertained that possibility. But it could be a meteorite, a bomb, an earthquake, a fire.

I unlocked my eyes from Tem's reflection and grabbed the real Tem. I clung to him as to a cliff, and he clung right back.

I counted ten tense seconds. The pulse in his neck.

"Should we—?" I said.

"What?" Tem said quickly, almost hopefully, as though I was about to propose a solution.

"I don't know," I said. "Go to bed? It's way past our bed-time."

"Bedtime!" Tem said as though I was hilarious.

11:54 p.m. on April 17, 2043. We are both alive and well. Yet I mustn't get ahead of myself. There are still six minutes remaining.

SOME POSSIBLE SOLUTIONS

The MyMan Solution

I'm not one to hide MyMan away in the intimate parts of the house, the bedroom, the bathroom, the places where interactions are most likely to occur. I like it when MyMan sits at the kitchen counter. I like it when he lies on the white leather couch.

People do judge you for it, though. If your MyMan is sitting there on the white leather couch when friends come over for nuts and martinis, they'll say, Jesus Christ! Is that really necessary. Please, spare us.

And even though you may stand up for yourself at first, even though you attribute their disgust at least in part to jealousy, after enough harassment (it's true, it's true, he's not wearing a scrap of clothing) you dismiss him, and he rises with his permanent slight smile—a very mysterious smile, an odd wondrous smile, lips parted just enough to let in a woman's tongue—and bumbles his way down the hallway behind his big ever-erect cock, his lean blue athletic form here and there bopping up against the walls (oh my, the length and strength of his legs!), because the ambulatory function hasn't yet been perfected (not that I'm complaining).

Then, after that, your friends can sit back and enjoy their martinis. Your loneliness doesn't seem to bother them in the least.

Well, *ha* to them! What I like about MyMan is his hard blue penis coupled with the outcropping above it that vibrates against my clit. I've never had this kind of experience before. He never goes soft, he never gets tired, boredom isn't in his register. In the months since I acquired him we've been coupling three, four, five times a day. There are serious health benefits, you know, to this sort of behavior. Seriously, they're visible. In my skin, primarily. You should see my face.

But that's not the only thing I'm talking about. Also I'm talking about his eyes. Twin mirrors reflecting me back at myself. What I've found extra beautiful these past months is when I can see myself in his eyes and then he blinks his lashless lids (every four seconds, programmed for verisimilitude) and I can't see myself and then he opens his eyes and I can see myself again.

And his arms. I'm talking about his arms. His hands. The sculpted plastic musculature, right down to the thick, visible veins running up his forearms. This plastic—it's not plastic as I've ever known it—there's something soft about it—so terrifically smooth—better than skin.

Afterward he holds me from behind, my bum pressed against the cool washboard of his stomach, and then if it happens to me again I can simply slide right back onto his cock. Let me just say: They must have interviewed hundreds of focus groups. They must have had teams of biologists. They got it so, so, so right. Down to the conversation. There's even something delightful about washing his penis with a sponge.

"Do you love fucking me?" I might say.

"I love fucking you," he's programmed to reply in his low, flat voice.

"Do you want to come over here?" I'll say.

"I want to come over here," he'll reply.

"I'm not tired," I'll say.

"You are not tired?" he'll ask.

"Let me take a shower first," I'll say.

"Let you take a shower first?" he'll ask.

MyMan is first generation (yes, I paid an arm and a leg, but I got two arms and two legs, as I like to say to my friends). Things will surely change, and improve, in later generations, and I can't deny that I'll probably be first in line to upgrade to a newer, better MyMan.

However: there's something about my MyMan. A few days ago, a malfunction surfaced; if I said "Do you love fucking me?" he'd reply, "You have to go to the bathroom?," still reacting to my previous statement. After I recovered from the shock and the uncanniness, I was touched. I didn't even pull out the owner's manual.

"I'm going to have breakfast now," I might say, and he'd say, "Let's go to sleep," and then at night, when I told him, "I had such a tiring day at work," he'd ask, "You are going to have breakfast now?"

The result was that I began to perceive a sense of will pulsing through his statements. I went out to buy him some clothes, designer jeans and cashmere, but MyMan is not proportioned for human clothing—is decidedly not suited to wearing anything at all. The jeans ended short on his long legs, his biceps strained the cashmere sweater's seams, not to mention certain insurmountable problems at the fly, which of course had to remain unzipped.

I laughed at him.

"This isn't really working, is it?" I said.

"You got me some clothes?" he said, stuck a few responses back.

"You're too handsome for clothes!" I told him, and it's true. His head bald, perfect, above flawless features, Yul Brynner times a hundred.

"I would like to try them on," he said.

"You crack me up, really you do," I told him, already imagining the statements being reflected back at me sometime soon. I am too handsome for clothes? I crack you up, really I do?

"The cashmere first?" he inquired.

Sitting him down on the bed, yanking the jeans off him, I reminded myself that I don't need what others need: I don't need to stroll down a street or beach holding hands, making strangers envious of what a happy handsome well-matched couple I'm half of. I've done all that already, folks. Live with someone long enough and you'll start to hate yourself. I loved every man I ever divorced. It's just too hard to be good all the time, to keep up with someone else's moods and dysfunctions.

But you know what was easy, super easy? Giving MyMan a second or two of a blow job when he was lying there, naked again. He'd never grab the back of my head and shove it deeper onto his dick. He'd never groan when I stopped.

You're kind of . . . obsessed, my friends like to say, pressing their molars together in that ungenerous way, slurping flax-seed and pineapple smoothies, clutching their big maroon leather purses. You could do so much better, they tell me. You're so skinny, your skin is practically golden, no one would ever guess you're over forty, you make a shitload of money and everyone wants a piece of you, plus you look like a fucking million bucks in that neon bikini. You're wasting your glamour years on that MyMan.

Often when they think I'm laughing with them, I'm actually laughing at them. Someday maybe they'll find their own solutions. Or, more likely, maybe not.

What I need: a blue man, a white apartment, a row of palm trees, meditation in the morning and evening preceded and followed and preceded and followed by orgasm.

But anyway. All of the above is just to say that right now I'm stuck in a preposterous moment: Some minutes ago I awoke from a sensual dream (the devil licked liquor from the impression between my breasts while on the sand slowly moving sphinxes circled a syringe), ready yet again for MyMan, reaching over to turn him on (pun intended), only to discover that his smooth plastic form was no longer there cupping me from behind. Worried, inordinately worried, about him, about my investment in him, I rushed out of bed, naked and panicking, ran down the long white hallway; there he was, sitting on one of the high white stools at the glossy white kitchen counter, emitting from somewhere deep inside the soft whir of malfunction, elbows on the counter, head drooping downward in this defeated way, looking for all the world like a tired husband.

So here we are—but am I going, hey, where's the box, can this MyMan be returned, where the hell did I put the receipt? Am I righteous with indignation that the verbal mishaps were indeed indicative of deeper problems with this particular MyMan? Do I feel as though I've been saddled with a lemon?

Poor creature. He can't deliver any line I haven't fed him.

"Are you sad?" I can't resist saying, though I know how he'll respond to that, just as I know how he'll respond when I say, "Are you okay?," "Is something wrong?," "Don't worry."

I should return him, I know I should, and I bet I will; I've always stood up for myself as a consumer.

Yet here we are, side by side on sleek stools in the night. Slowly, wearily, he raises his head (most human of gestures, I'm suddenly realizing), and it strikes me that all along his slight mysterious smile has in fact been a grimace, and when I look at his eyes I'm surprised to see that (due, I suppose, to the darkness of the night) they no longer appear to be mirrors reflecting me; instead, they're black walls blocking me from his interior.

"I am coming," he says eventually, "I am sad. I am okay."

Then he does something that's outside of any setting I read about in the owner's manual: he lets the lower part of his right arm fall down across the cool countertop, his palm upward and his fingers splayed.

"Something is wrong," he says. "Don't worry?"

And what I think to myself is: Sheesh. What I think to myself is: Here we go again. Even things with perfect cocks have terrible problems. Even nuns fall in love.

The Courage Solution

When my husband joins me in bed at two in the morning—after I've spent the evening alone, mashing potatoes, glazing carrots, flipping through books about how to improve chances of conception (avoid everything that helps you have fun in this life)—I pretend I'm still asleep as he tells the story of the beautiful young drunk woman who was sitting across from him on the subway, how she first complimented his shoelaces and second told him he was cute and third stood up and fourth pushed his head hard against the plastic wall and fifth kissed him on the mouth and sixth wrote something on the back of a receipt and seventh crumpled it up and eighth threw it at him: *I love you. M. XXX-XXX-XXXX.*

I moan as though mostly asleep, yet here I am in knots beside him (his flesh still chilled from the rainstorm that caught him between the subway and home), crippled by jealousy: if only I were as courageous as that young woman who kissed my husband on the subway.

What we needed, we realized, was a wife. You for sexual purposes, me for housekeeping purposes. So, because it was finally legal, we arranged a three-way marriage with this woman Anna. The palindrome seemed somehow appropriate.

Anna! What a wife she was.

On the wedding day she was all smiles, as though she couldn't have been happier. There's a picture of the three of us in front of City Hall, Anna and I holding our small bouquets of Gerber daisies, we newlyweds grinning at the dandyness of it all.

Anna, precious Anna. On the wedding night we stroked her. We wondered if our old double bed was too small, if we ought to get a queen, but Anna didn't mind. She said she enjoyed being squeezed in between us. She said she enjoyed having my tits on one side and your cock on the other.

That was the thing about Anna, she could talk so dirty but still seem so sweet.

You couldn't find a more generous wife than Anna. More than anything, she seemed so *happy,* as though spending the whole day cleaning the house and cooking dinner was some kind of divine meditation. There was this one line of organic cleaning products she totally loved, and even though the products were quite pricey we encouraged her to buy them, because we wanted Anna to have whatever she wanted, absolutely whatever she wanted; lavender was her favorite fragrance. She'd travel long distances on the subway to farmers' markets to purchase strange, dazzling local vegetables; she'd roast these vegetables in bizarre but brilliant combinations of spices. By the time we returned home from work, the candles would be lit and the table laid with the yellow napkins she'd bought to give our tired gray placemats new life (in addition to everything else, Anna had excellent visual taste). Scooping steaming vegetables from the pan, she'd ask in her dear way about our days, our failures and frustrations, encouraging us to see the minor successes amid our general sense of professional inadequacy. When we tried to reciprocate, asking about *her* day, she gently evaded the question, simply replying that it had been a good day, like every day.

All of which is not to mention what happened at night, in bed, where Anna was just as tidy, precise, fragrant, and eager to please as she was the rest of the time. Her breath smelled like cinnamon and her body was reminiscent of a seal's, sleek and shiny, with the perfect proportion of fat and muscle. Her face so symmetrical it would have made us feel bad about our own uneven faces if she hadn't been running her fingers so tenderly down our cheeks. Yes, she could stroke both of us at once, and indeed was always on the verge of orgasm herself.

Oh Anna. Our Lady of the Grocery List, Our Lady of the Linen Closet, Our Lady of Sorting Through the Junk Mail, Be Sure to Plug in Your Cell Phone, Don't Forget Your Umbrella, Here's the Lunch I Packed for You, Where Do You Want to Be Licked?

Our drawers were always filled with clean laundry, even our underwear folded. We, the people who used to shove our socks into the sock drawer without matching them up! Every corner of our home contained exactly what one needed at the instant one needed it: scissors, tape, last year's tax documentation. Whenever we misplaced something (The hat with the red pom-pom?), we simply had to ask Anna (Second box from the left at the top of the coat closet). Her mind was a library catalogue for our home. What a genius she was. How we adored her.

Yet it was hard to adore Anna. For instance, it was hard to think of a good gift for her. What did she love? She loved flowers, but she always bought them herself, at the farmers' markets, clutches of zinnias she put in the blue jug my cousin had given us for *our* wedding, arrangements that elevated our moods the moment we stepped in the door, and, on second thought, who knows whether Anna really loves flowers herself or if she just knew how we loved them? Yes, she loved organic cleaning products, but that's not something anyone can *love* love, plus it's not gift material. It upset her to think of us wasting our paychecks on clothing for her, on a fancy dinner for her, when she was so happy anyway, yet when her birthday came around we did give her a shiny blue dress and took her out, but she just sat there looking radiant and uncomfortable, moving her elbows on and off the black linen tablecloth of the fine, edgy restaurant we'd selected. She didn't drink and she didn't smoke and she got nervous riding the subway late at night. As soon as we returned home, she pulled out a lavender-scented SurfaceWipe and started to polish the bathroom floor, still wearing her new dress, and when we peeked in on her crouching there she looked up at us and smiled for the first time that night.

"Anna, Anna," we cried out, "Anna! Please, tell us, what can we do for you?"

But she just smiled in that quiet way of hers and squeezed out of the blue dress as she walked across the bedroom toward us, taking our breath away.

When we gave her a slender silver necklace, she thanked us profusely and wore it that evening but then we never saw it again. We could only speculate, during our brief time alone together each day, that she'd flushed it down the toilet or thrown it into a gutter. Of course far more likely was that it had somehow fallen off, that the clasp had broken and she, in her fathomless politeness, didn't want to mention it to us. Yet we were suspicious.

We encouraged her to rest on the weekends, to take a nap or come to the park with us or go see the mermaid parade. But she would only nap if we were napping too, and if it was one of those naked late afternoon "naps." We encouraged her to read books, we had lots of books plus we'd buy her any book she requested, we'd subscribe to any magazine, and we urged her to listen to music, to download the songs she liked, we could pay, we were happy to pay, and also she could be the boss of our Netflix queue. "Maybe a vegetarian cookbook would be nice," she said softly (we were both vegetarians). She was too busy, she often said, to do anything except keep house, and though she obediently tended to the Netflix queue, she was attentive only to our viewing history and the recommendations generated on the basis of our past favorites.

"Anna . . . what's your favorite movie, Anna?" we once asked her, desperately.

"Oh," she said with that infinite smile, "I don't have favorites."

Anna didn't make us feel guilty about the dishwasher we never had to unload or the toilet paper that never ran out. Yet that only increased our feeling of guilt. In the months before the divorce, we began to long for Anna to flare up, to scream at us that we were selfish and lazy and never lifted a finger, because it seemed inconceivable that we could receive all these blessings for free. We wanted to pay, pay, pay.

The Sniper Solution

There came a time in my life when I could not speak to another person without imagining that person's skull getting shot by a bullet on the left-hand side of his/her head, as though there was a sniper in the upper corner of every room I was ever in, a sniper crouched atop each building I passed.

The person (my husband or whoever else) would just be talking to me, innocently, and there I'd be, watching the explosion of bone and blood and brain and hair spraying out across the room or the bus or the street, speckling the person's clothing with red and other disturbing colors.

I would feel so tenderly toward the person just then, seeing the delicate inside revealed this way, the horrifying ketchup of it all, the imminent loss, and I would try to listen so closely, ever so closely, to what the person was saying, as though I was listening to his or her dying words.

"Oh my god," I would agree, "yes, yes, I see what you mean."

I could only hope this tic of mine had something to do with compassion, and with becoming a better person.

THE DOPPELGÄNGERS

The Queen always looked profound when she pooped. Her eyes solemn, as though regarding the void. That was why they had taken to calling her The Queen, even though she was only a month old. Also, the way she sat enthroned in her car seat in the over-packed car as they drove to the new town. And the regal purple stars on her blanket, beneath which her absurdly tiny legs jerked this way and that.

"It'll be better here," Sam assured Mimosa that night in the new house. She was standing in the new kitchen beside the new window looking out into the new backyard. She was holding The Queen close to her. She—Mimosa, not The Queen—was crying. The Queen was sleeping. The Queen's head fit flawlessly beneath Mimosa's chin. She wondered if all babies' heads fit so flawlessly beneath their mothers' chins, if it was a biological thing. Who were those women, those women who had cautioned her, "Don't worry if you don't love your baby right away; it takes a while"?

"It'll be better here," Sam said again, or maybe he didn't. She was too tired to know. Everything was a blur—the red numbers on the digital clock, the black hole of The Queen's mouth.

Sam came up behind Mimosa and did something, the bite on the back of her neck, his vampire move. It was a trick he'd discovered by accident, one night many years ago; they'd been rolling around in bed and somehow his teeth had found the skin there. He'd immediately let go and apologized. "No," she'd said firmly, giddily, realizing that now she could love him. "I mean, please. Do it again."

Since this was the first time he had done it since the birth of The Queen, Mimosa was particularly sensitive to it. The touch of his teeth traveled silken down her spine, like an epidural in the seconds before it begins to numb. She turned to him, opening her mouth. The Queen awoke with a howl.

While Sam was at work, Mimosa ran her fingers from the top of The Queen's head all the way down her spine, again and again, an addiction. It was too much, this beauty, this responsibility. The Queen burped. The Queen stared wide-eyed at the corner of the room as though watching a ghost emerge from the wall. The Queen farted. Mimosa couldn't bear the softness like a piece of overripe fruit where The Queen's skull had yet to fuse. It seemed that The Queen could vanish or disintegrate in an instant, that it would take almost nothing to destroy her.

"Are you there?" Sam said, standing in the doorway. A heat wave had begun. The bedroom was hot and dark. The whole house was hot and dark. He couldn't see who was crying and who was sleeping.

Over the weekend they did things. Nice things, together, as a family. Sam insisted. It felt strange to Mimosa to be out and about, strolling down the sidewalk, sitting on a bench, eating ice cream. She was so accustomed to being inside the house. She was so accustomed to sitting on the bed with The Queen on her knees. Her armpits were damp and her sundress smelled. Her breasts were leaking.

On the other bench, another couple ate ice cream and gazed into a stroller. The woman wore the same sandals as Mimosa.

"Let's go," Mimosa said, standing abruptly.

Sam looked up, surprised.

"Come on," she said.

The labor had been so long. She hadn't slept more than three hours at a stretch since then. He rose and gripped the handlebar of the stroller. She stormed down the sidewalk toward a quieter street. Small, sensible houses, not unlike their own. She allowed Sam and The Queen to catch up with her. At the end of the block, a woman was watering a row of sagging stargazer lilies with a long hose. Mimosa, who liked stargazers, very nearly smiled as they approached the yard.

But this woman, the woman with the hose; she was wearing

the same sundress as Mimosa. And, arcing outward from the small house: the wail of a newborn.

In the middle of the middle of the night, The Queen was screaming for milk, and Mimosa's breasts were dripping, but the screaming interfered with the latch. The Queen was sticky with milk. Mimosa was sticky with milk. Mimosa wrestled The Queen's confused, damp body closer to her nipple. Milk plastered them together at their stomachs.

On Monday, the heat was worse than ever. Something was happening to The Queen: hundreds if not thousands of small bumps had arisen on her skin. Mimosa noticed the rash when The Queen woke her at 4:57 in the morning (Sam slept through the crying, could always sleep through, and this was troubling to Mimosa, and at times filled her with queasy hatred, as though she had married a Frisbee or a spoon rather than a man).

Mimosa stepped around the moving boxes and turned on the overhead light in The Queen's room. She removed The Queen's onesie and diaper. She stood at the changing table for far too long, staring at The Queen's skin. The Queen kicked and twisted and reached, oblivious to her mother's hard gaze. Only when The Queen's flailing arm had a little heart-wrenching spasm (overexcitement? agitation?) did Mimosa finally pick her up.

She went back into the other room and watched Sam sleep. Then she shoved The Queen at his face.

"Look!" she commanded.

"Oh," Sam cooed sleepily, taking the baby, pressing her into his chest hair. "I am looking! I am looking at this beautiful, perfect baby! Oh my!"

The Queen smiled at her father, or so it seemed.

Mimosa pulled The Queen away from him and held her close, as close as close could be, the baby's head in its nook beneath Mimosa's chin, but she wished there was some way to hold her even closer.

The house felt small, small and hot. Mimosa could smell herself more strongly by the minute. Her body odor had intensified since The Queen's birth. Sam had read somewhere that newborns can recognize only one person in the entire world, and the way they recognize that person is by scent alone. She wondered when her stink would begin to offend The Queen, or if The Queen liked it more as it grew stronger.

In the car on the way to the park she felt victorious (having packed the diaper bag, located the car keys) and rolled down all the windows. She wanted to sit on a bench by the pond and hold The Queen in her lap and gaze at the swans. This was something she had imagined doing when she was pregnant.

But today even the birds terrified her. The swans and the pigeons were preparing for a face-off. They surrounded the most desirable bench, the pigeons viciously iridescent, the swans viciously white, ready for some kind of reckoning.

She spun the stroller around, away from the battlefield. The Queen began to fuss. Only a witch would dare stroll her infant in such indecent heat.

"You're my best friend," she said to soothe The Queen, but it just sounded plaintive.

Mimosa drove home slowly. She wished The Queen could be up front in the passenger seat beside her. She narrated the sights they passed: that's a church, that's a school, that's a gas station. Soon the backseat was swathed in the hush of The Queen's sleep. They said it was good to talk to your baby, but sometimes it was hard to know what to say, even when your baby was The Queen.

If Mimosa had been alone, truly alone, as she had so often been as of five weeks ago, she would have turned on the radio. But now the hush enveloped the car as Mimosa pulled up to a stop sign.

There were four cars at the four-way stop, three in addition to Mimosa's.

First the car to Mimosa's left passed through the intersection, driven by a woman with a dark bob, a tired face, a car seat in the back. Next the car to Mimosa's right passed through the intersection, driven by a woman with a dark bob, a tired face, a car seat in the back. Then the car across from Mimosa passed through the intersection, driven by a woman with a dark bob, a tired face, a car seat in the back. Now it was Mimosa's turn. She was horrified, paralyzed.

Yet it was her turn, and so she drove.

Early evening, and Sam was driving. A deep blue summer night, birdsong paired with silence. Stopped at a red light, they watched a woman push a stroller across the gleaming crosswalk.

"This town," Mimosa said bitterly as the light turned green.

"What?" Sam said.

There was a row of dark trees, the kind of trees that ought to be Christmas trees. They looked strange here, in the heart of the summer, standing upright against the heat.

"Filled with doppelgängers of me," Mimosa said. As she said it, she could see them—furrowing their brows the same way over the list of ingredients on a jar of tomato sauce, struggling the same way to wipe the shit out of the rolls of fat on their babies' thighs.

Sam gave half a laugh. Mimosa glanced back to check on The Queen. The backseat was dim, but she sensed that the baby was awake.

"Yeah," Sam said in that flat way of his. "That's why I love you. 'Cause you're just like everyone else."

She craned her neck further, caught a glimpse of her accomplice's dark alert eye.

Mimosa had been very organized, before all this. She'd had plans to start a small business. Somewhere on her computer there were spreadsheets.

"Just because they, what, have the same stroller we have?" Sam said as he pulled into their driveway.

He got out and opened the door to the backseat and unlatched The Queen. The Queen spat up on him, just as so many babies all over town were spitting up on their fathers.

It was eerie, more than eerie, it was nauseating, to see them standing at the gas station, their hair wilting in the heat just like hers, their bodies at the same stage of post-birth flab.

There was a doppelgänger in the produce section. Perched in the woman's shopping cart, a sleeping infant in a handy detachable car seat identical to the handy detachable car seat of The Queen. Mimosa hid behind the bananas and watched. The woman held a real lemon in one hand and a lemon-shaped container of lemon juice in the other. She dropped the lemon into her cart, put the container back on the shelf, and began to walk away. Then she turned around to swap the lemon for the container. Then, she changed her mind again, put the container on the shelf once more, and returned the lemon to her cart.

Mimosa recognized the indecision born of exhaustion, that familiar fuzziness. This sizzle of recognition propelled her toward the woman.

"I did that just last week," Mimosa found herself saying.

The doppelgänger, now studying the nutrition information on the container of lemon juice, didn't react. Boldly, Mimosa raised her voice a second time.

"I have a hard time choosing between them," she said. Her voice seemed an intrusion in the cool, tranquil supermarket.

The doppelgänger turned to her with a radiant smile, and Mimosa reacted with a radiant smile of her own.

"I know!" the doppelgänger said, as though they were in the middle of a conversation. "It's like, convenience versus authenticity. I can't believe that squeezing a lemon sounds like too much of a hassle, but that's just where I am in my life right now, you know?"

So much did Mimosa know that she had to blink back a pair of tears.

"How old?" the doppelgänger asked, turning her smile on The Queen.

"Six weeks," Mimosa said.

"Mine too!" the doppelgänger exclaimed. "Well, six and a half. Just started smiling for non-gas reasons last week. Look, you've got to join my moms' group for babies born in June."

"Oh," Mimosa said, revolted and fascinated.

"Mary Rogers," the doppelgänger said, sticking out her hand.

"Mimosa Smith," Mimosa said.

"Mimosa!" Mary Rogers said. "That's quite a name."

"My mom's favorite drink," Mimosa explained, as usual. Mary Rogers didn't yet know that, aside from her name, Mimosa was just like any other plain Jane.

It was there, damp with sweat, in the pocket of her sundress. She reached down and squeezed it during dinner. She'd made pasta and now she didn't know why she'd made something that required water to boil. The night was already devastatingly hot.

"Want me to hold her?" Sam said across the small breakfast table. They had a dining room with a dining table, but they had yet to use it. Mimosa held The Queen with one arm and with the opposite hand clenched the piece of paper torn magnanimously from Mary Rogers's shopping list. On one side, Mary Rogers had scrawled the name of the café where the moms' group was meeting this week; on the other side, *brown rice, prune juice, paper towels, oli-*. It felt so intimate to have this scrap from another woman's list, her items jotted just as messily as Mimosa's always were.

Mimosa insisted on holding The Queen, even though the baby's warmth was increasing her own temperature by a degree or two.

"You need to eat your food," Sam said.

The Queen is my food.

"It was stupid to make pasta in this heat," she said.

Sam shrugged, pressed a forkful into his mouth. She could tell he agreed.

"Let me take the baby," Sam said, "so you can eat."

She pitied him, and willed herself to pass the baby. The Queen kept it together for twenty seconds before starting to shriek. He stood up, bounced her, didn't do it quite right. Mimosa refrained from critiquing his technique. They couldn't be put into words, anyhow, The Queen's particular needs. After a few minutes he was forced to return the baby to her mother. The Queen quieted instantly, offensively. Sam carried the plates to the sink and put them down hard.

The women threatened to overwhelm the café, these women with their strollers and sandals and sundresses, staked out at two large tables and encroaching upon a third. Mimosa struggled through the doorway with her stroller. She was stuck halfway in, halfway out, when it occurred to her that she could still escape. It could still be just her and The Queen, alone together.

"Hi! Welcome!" one of the doppelgängers cried out—

Mary Rogers, she assumed, though it was impossible to know. "Come on over!"

And they all turned their heads, their tired faces reflecting her tired face. They were gesturing to her, they were scooting aside to make room.

For the first time in a long time, Mimosa knew exactly what was required of her. She glided across the café and took her place among them. She was given a seat and an iced tea. She pulled The Queen out of the stroller and began to nurse her, idly, as the others were. So this was all she had to do: sit here, nurse her baby, blend in.

But then the questions began. *How many weeks? Where'd you deliver? Pounds, ounces? How'd you pick the name? When do you go back to work? Have you figured out child care? What's the nap schedule? Sleeping much at night yet?* So flustered did she become that she said the wrong birth date, the tenth instead of the twelfth, but was too embarrassed to correct the mistake, because one of the doppelgängers had already gone into raptures about the fact that her baby had been born on the same day.

Mimosa took shelter in the sight of The Queen—until she observed that the rash had now spread to the scalp. She hoped none of the other mothers would notice.

"We were just saying how much wet wipe dispensers suck," someone said. "We can go to the moon, but we can't create something that makes it easy to get those fucking wipes out?"

She'd had this same thought two days ago, struggling to yank them out while holding The Queen's kicking legs high above her gooey diaper.

"So," someone said to Mimosa. "How've you been holding up?"

They were all looking at her. The answer was on the tip of her tongue: *Oh, just fine.* She gazed around the table, at all these other infants in various stages of sleep and wakefulness, of dissatisfaction and contentment. She had to admit that each of them was as beautiful as The Queen, and as repugnant.

"I cry two to four times a day," Mimosa said.

Her confession was met with silence. She shriveled. It was wrong to bare one's soul.

"Only four?" someone said.

"Try six!" someone yelled.

"Every time I go walking with the baby in the park, it's like someone turned on a fucking faucet."

"The other day this old lady in a wheelchair rolled up to me and was like, 'Are you okay? Can I help you?'"

"Oh my god, there's poop on my dress."

"Want half of my croissant?"

"Hey, please don't look too close at my baby, ladies! His rash is disgusting!"

"What are you doing?" Sam said one morning, coming up behind her.

Mimosa was standing at the mirror in the bathroom, gazing at herself, searching for the doppelgängers' faces in her own.

"Getting ready," she said. "Brushing my teeth."

But she was not brushing her teeth.

"Ready for what?" he said.

"To go and see the—" Mimosa stopped herself, then chose her word: "moms."

She regarded him coolly in the mirror, the same way she knew the doppelgängers regarded their husbands when asked what went on at all of those endless meet-ups.

In the nursery, The Queen coughed, whimpered. Mimosa felt as though her own arm was coughing, whimpering. She smiled to herself.

"Didn't you see them yesterday?"

Mimosa reached around him to pull her sundress off the hanger dangling from the hook on the bathroom door.

Yes, she had seen them yesterday, had sat with them in a circle, their assorted tears falling onto small heads encrusted with yellowish cradle cap. How precious they were, these women who believed their babies were tiny pieces of cosmic fluff the universe had blown their way for safekeeping, who despised themselves for being unfit for the endeavor of motherhood. There among the doppelgängers, you could come right out and say it: "I think I'm a witch." And they would echo you word for word. You could confess that in a recent dream you were turning into a geode, and the doppelgängers would list all the things they'd dreamed they were turning into. They knew the feeling—love enwrapped in dread—that made it difficult to push the stroller down the street without being overwhelmed by dark daydreams of garbage trucks rearing up onto the sidewalk.

She hummed a lullaby as she buckled her sandals. Sam watched her. He had gotten The Queen out of her crib, but The Queen wanted her mother.

Mimosa stood up and spread her arms wide.

Sam, again. Across the table. Nighttime now. Hair unruly, unshaven: a stranger. They were eating summer squash but it tasted mealy, as though the summer had gone on far too long.

"I feel bad for us," Sam said.

Mimosa stayed quiet, as she so often did nowadays, except when she was among them. At tables all around town, weren't the other mothers also feeling the weight of their own little lives? She was addicted to eating dinner with The Queen in her lap, but it was difficult to wield the forkfuls of squash so that no chunks fell down onto The Queen's painfully soft hair.

The Queen wiggled her legs, unrolled her crooked little sidelong smile.

Mimosa willed herself to reach across the table and touch Sam's forearm. She stroked his veins with all the tenderness she could muster. He stared down at her hand as though it was five worms rather than five fingers.

The Queen's smile flipped; a wail began deep inside her and shot upward.

"What's her problem?" he said. The question sounded harsh, but he was asking it the way a little boy would—scared, and truly wanting to know the answer.

In the black of the night, Mimosa reached out toward Sam's silhouette, but there was nothing there. She could see his outline in the darkness, very dimly, his head on the pillow, but there was no body to touch.

Waking up sometime later to nurse The Queen, she saw

that Sam was back, his outline and his body both—relieved, tender, she ran her fingers from the top of his head down his spine.

They were lounging on blankets in the park, the doppelgängers and their babies; the mothers were eating grapes, they were tossing grapes, they were laughing, their minds were loose and hazy, their babies had awoken them at 11 p.m. and 1 a.m. and 3 a.m. and 4:30 a.m. and 6 a.m., and what could be more hilarious than that? Now the babies were crying, now pooping, now wanting milk, milk, *milk*, and out came the luminous breasts, and who wouldn't want to place lips on breasts so full, and the mothers grinned at each other like a bunch of teenagers on the same high, and the heat wave painted an extra shimmer over it all, and the grapes were radiant in the grass and The Queen smiled her wide milky smile and motherhood (the doppelgängers agreed) was underrated, everything so dazzling, Mimosa had diamonds for eyes. A universe away from the grim dinner table in her quiet home, from the version of herself that had sat on a beat-up brown couch with Sam a decade back, both of them stock-still and united in secrecy when his ex-girlfriend entered the room; now it was she and The Queen who froze when he entered the room.

"Isn't it funny," one of the doppelgängers murmured lazily, "that we never talk about our so-called better halves?"

It was explosive, the chorus of agreement; it always was, with the doppelgängers. And Mimosa joined in; hadn't she just been marveling at her distance from him?

Yet amid the sharing that followed, the echoes upon echoes upon echoes, the dark amusement at their collective indifference to their partners, Mimosa found herself wanting Sam, she found herself standing up, drunkenly gathering The Queen's scattered belongings.

She dumped The Queen into the stroller, moving more hastily by the second, and set off across the grass toward the path, putting distance between herself and the smell of their laundered and spat-up-upon sundresses, fleeing the perfect alignment of their thoughts and her own.

She glanced back; the doppelgängers were all packing up and dispersing.

Back from the park, navigating through the screen door into the kitchen, Mimosa felt weak, awkward. The car seat banged hard against the door frame and The Queen awoke with a shriek, her body rigid in its devotion to the screams.

She clutched the writhing baby and ran down the hallway to the bathroom and hit the switch and stared at the mirror. The Queen's rash was worse than ever, spreading across her face; Mimosa felt it pressing upward as though through her own pores.

But meanwhile The Queen's screeching self was warm and strong, tried and true, and Mimosa couldn't contain all these sensations, the overlapping positive and negative and positive and negative. There was no room in her for such love; it was explosive, almost identical to panic.

She slammed the light switch downward. In the darkness, The Queen quieted. The desolate evening twined itself around them. Mimosa wondered what they looked like in the black mirror.

Sam.

"I'm beat," she confessed.

"I'll take the baby," he said. "You take a nap."

"What about dinner?" she said.

The Queen was limp, gentle, in his arms. Mimosa walked to the bedroom and plummeted into sleep.

When Mimosa awoke, she felt strangely refreshed, as though she had slept for years. The bedroom was cool, the heat wave broken. She couldn't wait to see them.

The house was dark. The car was gone. Outside, the last of the day was draining away swiftly, as it does in late August—or, wait, had September arrived?

She called out for them, even used The Queen's given name, but the words felt foreign on her lips.

The kitchen was invisible, silent.

It was no wonder that he had left her. She had been awful to him, hadn't she? Yet she couldn't remember how she'd been. All she remembered from the entire summer was The Queen's face, its thousand different expressions.

She didn't want to have to survive without him, but she could.

The other, though—that she could not survive.

There was only one place she could think of to go. In the ever-weakening light, she hurried down sidewalks no one ever walked. She couldn't tell where the night ended and she began.

Approaching the house, Mimosa anticipated a scene identical to the one she'd fled: Mary Rogers standing alone in her own unlit kitchen, orphaned. But when she looked through the screen door, she saw that Mary Rogers's kitchen was all Technicolor—the brilliant red of the tablecloth, the intense white gleam of the refrigerator. There sat Mary Rogers, glorious, at the small breakfast table in the corner, beneath the glow of an orange plastic shade, with her husband and her baby. They were just finishing dessert. Mary Rogers held the baby—almost but not quite as beautiful as The Queen. Mary Rogers's husband's back faced Mimosa. It could have been Sam's back—the post-work slump, the hair just beginning to dull.

Mimosa wanted, more than she had ever wanted anything, to slip into Mary Rogers's body, hold her baby, eat her last spoonful of ice cream.

Mary Rogers stood and passed the baby to the husband. As she turned to walk out of the kitchen into the hallway, Mimosa noticed the mouth-shaped marks on the back of her neck.

When Mimosa pressed, the screen door into Mary Rogers's kitchen opened with a squeak she recognized from her own screen door.

"Well hello," said Mary Rogers's husband with an odd matter-of-factness. He twisted around to smile at her.

He looked just like Sam.

The baby on his lap began to whimper. She felt her milk come down. Her fingertips went electric with desire. She rushed across the kitchen and seized the baby. The man's only protest was a wry half-laugh.

"Oh baby," she said. "Where'd your mama go?"

She sat down across from him and unbuttoned her sundress. The baby latched. That ecstatic buzz of oxytocin; she could feel it spreading through her blood, making her toes and fingers tingle, opening the valves of her heart and the ducts in her breasts, a downpour of milk and sympathy.

He watched her in that flat, cool way of his. She enjoyed his gaze. She felt grand, maternal, untouchable, like a woman from before human history.

When the baby had taken its fill, she buttoned her sundress and stood up, holding the baby close, its head in the nook beneath her chin. He too stood and they stepped away from the breakfast table, out of the circle cast by the hanging lamp.

He placed his forehead against her forehead.

"What if she comes back?" she said.

"Who?" he said. His breath on her eyelid. "Who are you talking about?"

THE MESSY JOY OF THE FINAL THROES OF THE DINNER PARTY

Eva was in the kitchen, placing a pile of dirty dishes beside the sink, when a silence fell across the dinner table in the other room, the deep silence of people waiting for someone to pull a photograph of his child out of his wallet—or, more likely, waiting for a YouTube video to load. Moments before, there had been escalating banter about the sexual indiscretions of a once-beloved politician and the dubious merits of an art-house film. Frankly, it had been a relief to escape to the kitchen, to scrape the nauseating scraps into the trash can. She hid behind the idea that she alone had carried the dirty plates into the kitchen because she alone was a gracious dinner guest—a pleasing alternative to her knowledge that she alone had carried the plates into the kitchen because she alone did not belong here, among these dazzling, merciless people.

Eva embellished her good-guesthood, rinsing the plates, lining them up in the dishwasher, all the while waiting for the silence to break, for a roar of laughter to pummel outward. Yet the silence held, and it became clear to Eva that she'd have to reenter the other room.

Stepping through the doorway, she couldn't contain her gasp of shock. What an odd, odd joke for them to play on her—all seven of them frozen in place, the host half-standing to pour cream into coffee, forks held in various positions between apple pie and mouth, a hand thrown upward in emphasis, a head thrown backward in laughter, fingers wrapped fervently around wineglasses: a flawless tableau of the messy joy of the final throes of the dinner party.

She tiptoed toward the table, waiting for them to break scene, turn toward her with faces that demanded the correct response. Yet the tableau remained utterly perfect, still, disconcerting. Eager to catch a blink, Eva stared at the eyelids—and realized that most were halfway or three-quarters open or closed, stuck at different stages of a blink.

She turned her attention to the host, the exact sort of no-nonsense All-American handsome that was never attracted to her. It was then, gazing at the cream he was pouring, that she understood: the cream, suspended in its arc, absolutely unmoving, its white tip just barely touching the dark surface of the coffee.

This was no joke, no performance. Everything was frozen. Except for her.

She lifted her hand, waggled her fingers in her host's face. No response.

At that point her terror should have overwhelmed her. But what she felt was glee.

First she walked over to her husband, her beloved unshaven husband, he whose eyes were nearly shut as he drank deep from a glass of red wine. She kissed him on the forehead, stroked his cheek; a strange place to start, perhaps, in this roomful of seven, with the one person she actually had the right to touch. But he wasn't always amenable to having his face stroked or his forehead kissed.

Next, back to the host, he who enjoyed his opinions. Eva seized this opportunity to put her lips against his, giving him and all his fraternity brothers a one-sided kiss.

Eva removed her hostess's necklace—she'd had her eye on it all evening—and slung it around her own neck. It was a large metal pendant on a black string, the kind of object that could protect you. Then, Eva removed the eyeglasses of the librarian—she who took pleasure in wearing thick eyeglasses, knowing how her sharp beauty transformed them—and placed them on the gooey plate beside her delicately bitten pie. As for the hostess's overweight but witty sister (it was easy to imagine a childhood of despair): Eva removed the woman's rubber band and reworked her ponytail, putting it at a cocky angle, helping her capitalize on her thick hair, the one thing she had over her sister. The graduate student, so young and tired-looking, merited the same treatment as Eva's own husband: the kiss on the forehead, the stroke of the cheek.

Eva paused in her labors to stick her finger into the freshly whipped cream, something she'd been desperate to do ever since her hostess placed it on the table. She wanted to eat it forever and ever—but duty called.

The two remaining men were indistinguishable from each other. They'd been egging the conversation along all night, mocking or interrogating anyone who made any kind of definitive statement about anything. What *were* their names? Fred and Ted, Tom and Ron, Tim and Jim? Yet they seemed ever so much less irritating now that they were stuck here with their mouths open to receive forkfuls of pie. Gently, she sprinkled salt.

Her work complete, Eva stepped back to admire them, this small group of immobile human beings, all of whom had traveled through life to arrive at this dinner table. All of whom felt unloved and lonely and stupid and awkward and guilty and anxious and insufficient, all of whom woke up each day and did things, tried to do the right things, brushed their teeth and attempted not to shame themselves, took pride in their little accomplishments and strove to speak with authority about a thing or two. How vulnerable they looked now, trapped in their humblest gestures, how pitiful, how dear! She found herself achingly aware of their skeletons, of the fact that just beneath their skin lay tendons and intestines and other repulsive things. She loved them, these people—the lettuce lodged in someone's tooth, the parade of acne across a forehead, the stain on the shirt, the fray of the hem.

She returned to the host, stuck in the most unnatural position of all. She knew he'd felt as out of place the whole evening as she had; she knew everyone had felt as out of place the whole evening as she had.

It was just then, as she was moving her lips once more toward his, that it broke.

Suddenly they were sipping, biting, pouring, breathing. And then they were staring at her, blinking at her, because *what* was she doing all up in the host's face when he was trying to pour the cream? And, excuse us, but why's she got the hostess's Peruvian charm around her own neck?

And then the interchangeable men spitting salty pie into their napkins, the perplexed librarian salvaging her glasses from her pie goo, the fat sister's hand searching for her relocated ponytail, the hasty return of the necklace to the hostess, someone wondering aloud who dared stick his finger into the whipped cream, the kind yet slightly ashamed gaze of her beloved husband. Serene, Eva strolled around the table and settled into her seat, from whence she had a perfect view.

LIFE CARE CENTER

Across the hall from the room where my sister may or may not be dying, there is a woman who moans *Help* all day long.

Should we help her? I eventually ask my parents.

Help who? my father says.

The woman who keeps saying *help*, my husband says.

No, she doesn't need any help, my mother says.

What lovely sunflowers, I say. What lovely orchids. How kind.

Have you sanitized your hands? my mother says. You have to sanitize your hands.

Orchids and sunflowers, I say. They look surprisingly good together, don't they.

At first we too wanted to help the woman who says help, my father says, but the nurses told us she says it all day every day.

You know, they're sort of perfect opposites, orchids and sunflowers, I say.

Are you guys hungry? my father says. There are chocolates over there.

Did you have anything on the plane? my mother says.

Isn't it hard to believe you woke up in Brooklyn this morning and now you're here in Colorado, my father says.

Hey, she smiled! my husband says. Look, she's smiling.

Oh wow, my father says. Great. Wow. Look at that.

Hi there girl, I say.

Smiley smiley girl, my mother says. You're smiling because you know your little sister and her boyf—husband flew all the way across this great big country to visit you, aren't you, girly-girl?

You had us scared, you know that, I say.

Thank you for smiling, precious, my mother says.

On the TV, the barn-raising scene in the musical *Seven Brides for Seven Brothers.* Six brothers in their bright shirts dance on a sawhorse. My father and my husband crank my sister's hospital bed to the full upright position.

A confession: I have never looked into my sister's eyes and seen there anything that resembled recognition. Sometimes when we were children I would accidentally call her by the dog's name—*Hush-a-bye, Freck!* I might say when she moaned—before quickly correcting myself, hoping my parents hadn't heard.

In bed, the smiley girl smiles.

In the newly opened café across the highway from the Life Care Center, there are thirteen varieties of dessert on the other side of the glass case: rhubarb bread pudding, peach pie, apple pie, chocolate cake, carrot cake, cinnamon rolls, chocolate chip cookies, oatmeal raisin cookies, cranberry scones, lemon bars, almond croissants, chocolate croissants, chocolate cupcakes. *Everything baked on the premises! Including the ciabatta!*

Awed, genuinely awed, we ask the owner: *How* do you do it all? She does it single-handedly. She has red hair and big yellow teeth. She says: Well if you want to know how I do it is for say the pie I would make a bunch of pastry dough and then freeze it and save it for when I needed to make a new pie like today I made eighteen piecrusts or if you're wondering about the scones what I do is I make a huge batch of scone batter and then save it in the fridge and then when I want fresh scones well all I do is pull some out and throw in walnuts or what have you I make ten batches of say chocolate chip cookie dough and shape it into balls and freeze them and then every morning I just throw a few on a cookie sheet so we have fresh-baked cookies basically I just rotate like this morning I made eighteen piecrusts it's all about rotating almond ganache can keep for weeks . . .

By the time she finishes explaining everything we have finished our mushroom soup and our ciabatta. Already we are imagining ourselves standing up, walking to the door, stepping out into the parking lot of the strip mall, getting into the car, going back across the highway, returning to the person who has not eaten anything for sixteen days. Already we are nauseous. The owner's teeth are so yellow. As we leave she forces us to sample her lemon bar—I sliced it into four pieces, one for each of you! What do you think! What do you think of my lemon bar! The tang flips around in our hot mouths, burned from the mushroom soup.

After lunch the old people are lined up in the hallway of the Life Care Center. They all sit there in their wheelchairs, big around the crotches due to diapers. Some of them stand out. A woman who is bald but for a hundred white hairs. A man whose skin is so pale he looks dead. I can't believe they let a dead man sit there alongside the others! A woman strapped to her wheelchair with twelve bright orange straps. A woman with an eager smile who says to everyone walking by, Did you bring it today? Did you bring it? A man who is able to ask us, How is she doing? and to whom we are able to reply, She is finally eating again.

Yet these distinctions between the old—perhaps they are mostly imagined. In truth they are lined up there in the hallway like one enormous, indistinguishable beast that smells of urine and overcooked fish.

Passing them is like passing down a gauntlet. We cannot decide if it is better to avert our eyes or to smile. We cannot tell if they are staring at or through us. Do they know that they are old, and that they stink?

It's like something from a fairy tale: Once upon a time, in the castle of the ancient ones. At least this is what we try to tell ourselves.

My sister does not exactly belong here. She is five decades younger than the others who live in the rooms lining this hall. Yet she is retarded enough to fit in. (Please don't use that word. Please don't even think it.) Yet she is (handicapped? disabled? crippled?) enough to fit in. Yet she is ________ enough to fit in. Like them, she cannot walk. Cannot feed herself. Wears diapers. Sickens easily. Is prone to fatal pneumonia. Because she cannot talk, we have nothing to await aside from her smiles. This can cause boredom, impatience.

Yet she is magical enough to fit in. Yet she is mystical enough to fit in. A beautiful anomaly in the stinking castle of the ancient ones.

Before she was quarantined in her room, the old folks fawned over her, or so the nurses tell us.

Once upon a time, a beautiful young woman married a handsome young man. They had a splendid baby girl, but the baby was cursed.

Here's what happened: the baby girl was born normal—perfect, precious, flawless, adorable, charming, cute, cuddly, lovely, sweet, dear, darling, delightful, beautiful, winsome, bonny—but just before her first birthday she forgot the few words she had learned. Her legs went limp. Her eyes crossed. Her hands wrung. Her tongue lolled.

It was difficult to get excited about the offspring that followed.

(A medical explanation, please? Eventually the girl was diagnosed with Rett syndrome. Reye's syndrome? No, *Rett* syndrome. Tourette's syndrome? No, *Rett syndrome.* Like Rhett Butler? Sure, minus the *h.* I've had Rhett syndrome my whole life! So, what is it? A neurological disorder occurring in one in twenty thousand live female births. Only girls? They're born completely normal, then stop progressing. Life expectancy? Unknown. Likely causes of death? Pneumonia; compromised lung function due to scoliosis and difficulty swallowing.)

Now, my husband and I are identical to what my parents were then. Just as beautiful, just as hopeful. *Newlywed.* A buoyant word.

I have no appetite here.

It smells like pee. My hair smells like pee.

It could happen to us.

We wish to bestow upon my parents a possible night from three decades ago. Make them young again. Put them on our cheap sun-stained couch. Wrap them around each other. Interweave their fingers. On TV, a black-and-white movie. In mugs, thick hot chocolate. October darkness beyond the window. The warm weight of an Indian blanket.

Her favorite movie: *Seven Brides for Seven Brothers.*
Her age: 29 years, 26 days.
Number of calories consumed today: 225.
Description of solid waste produced today: One marble-sized, green-brown.
Description of liquid waste produced today: Two diaperfuls of dark yellow urine.

At the Vietnamese restaurant, ravenous, the four of us raise our water glasses.

Gloriously we celebrate minuscule miracles: the consumption of over 200 calories, the emergence of a tiny turd, the upturn of half the mouth in a ghost of a smile.

A spring roll. A vegetable pot. A peanut curry. Brown rice. All so easy to eat. We have no trouble chewing anything and no trouble swallowing it either.

Then my father says: "No parent should have to prepare for the death of a child."

His head heavy in his hand, his elbows at odd angles on the table.

A glass of beer, close to empty. The beer flat, ungolden, mostly saliva.

My mother misplaces her expensive sunglasses at the Vietnamese restaurant. At a time like this, such a loss should be a matter of indifference, yet instead it contributes to the sensation that soon absolutely everything will be lost.

My husband and I insist on spending the night. My parents must be relieved; this is why we have come, to relieve them. The nurses wheel in a small bed. It has a pink polyester coverlet. We have to wear long sleeves to protect ourselves from the scratchiness of this coverlet. We have to sleep on top of each other. Every two hours they come in. They check the IV. They make sure she hasn't fallen out of bed. Not that she could. It affords her a certain dignity, that they treat her as though she might be capable of propelling herself out of bed.

Help: the lady across the hall stays up all night just to say it.

My husband whispering: The sound of your sister's limbs rustling against the sheet. That's the same sound as anyone's limbs rustling against a sheet. In the dark there's no difference between her and you.

This should be called the Death Care Center.

God it's hot in here isn't it?

Actually I'm cold.

The morning nurse says the night nurse said she'd never seen two such beautiful young people sleeping.

My husband and I escape to the grocery store across the highway, where we stand at the magazine rack flipping through shiny magazines, entranced by the glimmering faces. We have to rip ourselves away.

Upon our return we pass through the gauntlet of old people lined up in the hallway after breakfast.

There go the young ones, the dead man says.

The others nod; or perhaps they don't. God it smells like urine.

Maybe it is not that they are a gauntlet but rather that we are a parade.

In my sister's room, the sunflowers have blown over in a midmorning wind. Water all over everything. The floor treacherous. In bed, my sister kind of smiles.

On the TV, the climax of *Seven Brides for Seven Brothers. Come on, everyone! Milly—Milly's havin' her baby!*

Helen! someone is saying out in the hallway. Helen! But this person, thank god, is not talking to me. Helen! Come back! This way! Your room is this way, not that way! Helen glides slowly past the doorway with her walker. Her head stooped over to rest atop her low breasts. She is wearing a tracksuit of forest green velveteen, a material that belongs in a fairy tale. This way, Helen! This way! I am comforted by the kindly, persistent nurse who keeps repeating my name. Bless that nurse, and bless Helen.

My father's exhaustion expresses itself as a bony lump on each shoulder, his skeleton beginning to show.

My mother's exhaustion expresses itself via the capillaries in her eyes, which are, quite literally, bloodred.

I wish they were my own two children. I would bake them pies, put them to bed.

And the boredom. A half-teaspoon bite, wait forty-five seconds, watch for the swallow. A half-teaspoon bite, wait forty-five seconds, watch for the swallow. An hour and a half for the consumption of 200 calories. Don't underestimate the tedium.

Walking around the nearby lake we see two boys throwing rocks at ducks. We see lake grasses that are red, purple, orange. We see a man torturing three fish. There's nothing wondrous in life.

An error in the feeding process could be fatal. The pathways inside her are frequently confused, the muscles of the throat slow to react. Food slips easily into her lungs, where it rots.

Across the highway, a National Historic Landmark. A covered wagon, a homestead. Our shy tour guide barely dares speak a word. In the main room we run our hands over the huge logs. We learn that originally mud and honey were used to seal the cracks—replaced now, of course, by concrete. There are many large stone fireplaces, and an entire room devoted to the craft of spinning wool. I attempt this, a girl in a fairy tale, gingerly, my foot on the pump and my fingers on the wheel, trying to please the softly smiling tour guide, trying to please my father, my husband, trying to make this day feel normal, delightful, this tour something more than a distraction.

Back at the Life Care Center, my mother gets bored.

In the old-fashioned print shop we come upon thousands of small metal letters with which any book at all could be written.

Once upon a time, there was a magical building where the very oldest people lived. The final ritual in every wedding ceremony consisted of the young couple walking down the hallway of this building, which was lined with all the old people sitting in their special chairs. Each old person would bestow upon them a blessing, and the newlyweds would emerge into the dusk stronger, richer, and happier than before. During the wedding night their skin and hair would be redolent of ancient urine, and in the morning they would walk together to the gleaming river where they would wash each other. For the rest of their lives, the fragrance of urine would always remind them of abundance, ecstasy.

Do we make the old folks envious or joyous? Did Helen ever find her room?

We're not supposed to help them, you know.

They once had jobs and friends. It sounds miraculous, but it must be true. They once wore clothing that wasn't soft and forgiving.

Back at the beginning of *Seven Brides for Seven Brothers*, the eldest brother has just convinced Milly to marry him. He convinced her while she was milking the cow, leaning her cheek up against the warm barrel of its stomach.

My mother says: I've watched the first fifteen minutes of this movie twenty times in the last week.

Our grief is about ourselves. Our own regrets. Our own shortcomings.

As kids, we watched this movie uncountable times. Soon they will get married; they will ride the wagon up into the mountains; Milly will learn that he has six filthy brothers; Milly will teach those brothers some manners. I know every sentence in this movie yet I am not sick of it. In fact, I feel curious about what will happen next.

But we must leave. Plane to catch, et cetera.

Across the hall: *Help*.

A desire to watch *Seven Brides for Seven Brothers* in its entirety—regret about not being able to do so—we linger until Milly forces the brothers to remove their long underwear—until she trains them to court girls—until the barn-raising scene, again. The smiley girl may not see me again before she goes, but she will see this movie many times. Suddenly she looks away from the TV screen and stares straight into my eyes.

Suddenly you look away from the TV screen and stare straight into my eyes, absolving or interrogating or thanking or begging or parting. Why are you doing this? You never do this.

A confession: When we were kids and people asked how much you understood, I said "Everything," as I had been trained, but when I became an adult and people asked how much you understood, I said "Nothing."

Don't worry; I saw the recognition in your eyes when you stared at me. The unmistakable recognition. It left me shaking.

Now you will be stuck here forever watching *Seven Brides for Seven Brothers* in a darkening room, *Help* across the hall, eternally contemplating the scene just after the barn-raising scene, the scene from which I must tear myself away, regret for leaving you manifesting itself as regret for not watching the rest of the movie.

What can she do? my husband asked long before he was my husband.

She can smile.

Anything else?

She can cry.

Anything else?

Making it to the doorway, the golden threshold, rushing back.

An immobile girl alone in a darkened room. *Seven Brides for*

Seven Brothers in a darkened room. Cheerful song, cheerful song, cheerful song.

Out walking on a faraway dirt road. He and I, side by side. Night coming, yet the sky still white, the air still pink. Colors somehow brighter as the world begins to dim. An aster, a horse. A fistful of grass. The expectation of constellations, wood smoke. Hollow and weary.

In the distance, an incredible creature. As large as a baby elephant, with tan fur like a wooly mammoth. Some kind of magical beast moving through the twilight. Surprise, followed by terror. But this—this thing turns out just to be two people, a man and a woman, walking several paces apart in the darkening world.

THE JOINED

The pretty astronaut strolls in a landscape reminiscent of Earth, except the dirt is purple, the sky yellow, and the grass red. Aside from these details, we are reminded of the medieval hamlets we once learned about in our textbooks. She winds through a meadow, approaching a cluster of thatched cottages. Her movements are stiffened by the space suit, but still we can tell she is graceful. When she reaches the village, she finds a small crowd of aliens gathered in the central square. These aliens are much more like humans than anyone would have expected. Their skin comes in various shades of tan and brown. They wear dresses and pants. There are old ones, babies, children, couples, as on Earth. In fact, they resemble humans almost exactly, except that—well, how to say it? They're somehow vaguer around the edges. A bit blurry. It's hard to feel entirely confident about where their bodies end.

They seem to be gentle creatures. They smile at the astronaut with lips no different from our own. It's clear they would like to touch her, but they are polite and hold back. The mothers restrain their children. The old people hang on to one another's trembling hands. A strong young girl lowers a bucket into the well and carries it, overflowing, to the astronaut, who does not take it. Perhaps she wants to maintain the seal of her helmet. Perhaps she fears the substance offered may not be water. The girl isn't offended. She simply carries the bucket back to the well and dumps the unused fluid.

The astronaut seems touched. She gestures toward her heart. No one knew they would be so capable of charming us. She gazes at them, attempting to make eye contact with each. Her eyes meet those of a tall alien man on the outskirts of the group. He's as handsome as she is pretty. His stare is intense and tender.

She begins to wobble. He begins to wobble. She is elevated a few inches off the ground and her feet are dragged across the dry purple dirt, raising a cloud of lavender dust. The invisible force propelling her rapidly toward him also propels him toward her. The aliens step out of the way. A great black flash obscures the moment of encounter. The camera must have shattered, because this is all we have.

It's an amazing sight.

It is somewhat less amazing on the fiftieth viewing.

The TV networks become addicted to this footage

for the week following the incident. At first, we're addicted too.

"Look! Right there! In the middle of the black flash!"

"How can there be a black flash? Isn't a flash always white?"

"Did you see it this time?"

"See what? You're getting crumbs everywhere, by the way."

"What I told you to look for!"

"What?"

"In the middle of the black flash *there's a naked woman*! And a naked man too, but he's harder to spot. He's sort of—I don't know—misty."

"A naked woman? Scoot over."

"How can she be *naked*? She was wearing her space suit a millisecond ago."

"I don't know. I didn't see it."

"I *told* you to watch for it! Why do you never listen to me?"

"Mind if I have the last gingersnap?"

"Look, they're showing it again."

"Big surprise."

"*Look* for it this time, okay? *Look* for the naked woman. And next time round you can look for the naked man. You're not looking!"

"You're funny."

"Look really close. It's up there for like one-billionth of a second."

"Honey, you're funny."

"Are you watching?"

We mourn her. Wreaths of flowers are placed on the steps of the White House, as though it's the President who has lost someone he loved. There are magazine features and TV specials. We learn that the astronaut grew up on a farm in the Midwest and attended the Air Force Academy. We applaud her accomplishments.

After seven days, the astronauts get the camera up and running again. This means there's new footage: a male astronaut standing beside the silver leg of the spaceship and confessing to everyone on Earth that before this happened he'd been planning to ask the pretty astronaut to marry him. They'd been through so much together, what with the training and the journey and all. He weeps. The camera follows as he wanders despondent among the hills and dales of the new planet. He sighs, and on Earth we sigh. Lounging on the couch, we rub each other's feet.

He comes to a stream. The water shimmers gold. A young alien maiden is standing there, her skirt tied up around her knees and a jug in her hand. She stoops to touch a pink creature halfway between a frog and a cockroach that's sitting on a gray lily pad. The astronaut makes a noise, perhaps choking back a sob. She glances up at him, startled, and then it happens. The astronaut begins to wobble, and the girl begins to wobble. Some force rips her out of the water—golden flecks flying every which way—and up the bank. The same force tears him off his feet and straight into her.

Once again, the black flash.

On Earth, we grieve for the male astronaut. We imagine how

sweet it would've been if the two astronauts had returned to Earth and married each other.

This time, the astronauts fix the camera in only three days. But it's a subdued sight that meets our eyes. Only four of the original twelve crew members remain, huddled around the base of the spaceship. A middle-aged female astronaut with a gravelly voice explains that it's happened to six more.

"What do you mean, *it*?" The newscaster's voice crackles across the vastness.

"*It*," she says, widening her eyes. "*It*."

Just as we become certain she'll stand there silently staring until the cows come home, she whispers something. We strain to hear.

"*They're all very happy*."

Then she runs off into the woods, outside the scope of the unmanned camera.

Two days later, after forty-eight hours of footage featuring the least interesting crew members doing their daily business and avoiding questions about their lost shipmates, a strange creature ambles up to the camera while they're making dinner in the spaceship. This creature is kind of like—well, it's like two people back to back but with one torso and one head. The head has a face on either side, and two pairs of ears. Four arms and four legs. A single pair of buoyant breasts above the pearly little cunt, a tranquil dick on the opposite side. The creature's skin is tan and luminous.

We recognize the face of the pretty astronaut.

This is the face the creature turns toward the camera. She does not seem aware that the entire world can see her nipples, which are as exquisite as we'd all imagined.

"You have been lonely," she says. Her voice is deep and grand. We who have seen the TV specials recall the clips from her parents' home videos, in which she has a chirpy, if not squeaky, Midwestern voice. "You have existed as half of what you are. Please, come here. Be happy. Twe am."

"Twe?" we say, cocking our heads.

Willingly, the creature that was once the pretty astronaut allows its former shipmates to strap it into the Emergency Escape Capsule, which reaches Earth in a single week. When the creature arrives, it maintains its infinite calm while subjected to a battery of tests by doctors, psychologists, and NASA scientists. Countless images of the two smiling faces, the serene sexual organs, the thick legs and glowing skin, are delivered to our living room.

The face that used to belong to the pretty astronaut does all the talking, but a different brain seems to be at work. When her parents are brought into the room, the creature embraces them warmly. However, the creature warmly embraces everyone with whom it comes into contact. When the pretty astronaut's full Christian name is repeated time and time again, the creature emits a low melodious laugh, but it is not the laugh of recognition. When asked to describe its feelings, the creature simply claims, "Twe am happy."

"Well screw you," we say, throwing popcorn at the screen and wrapping the blanket tighter around ourselves.

A conference is held in Vienna, a gathering of our preeminent scientists and scholars. The creature attends; there are photos of it sitting in a chair especially crafted by an Austrian carpenter to accommodate its unusual shape.

After the conference, a distinguished professor comes on primetime television to announce that humankind has discovered the planet to which our split hermaphrodite ancestors were deported by Zeus several thousand years ago. The professor, gesturing at an oversimplified graphic consisting of two globes connected by many multicolored lines, explains that if the theories and equations resulting from the conference are correct, every single person on Earth has a corresponding being on the new planet to whom s/he can be joined, thus returning to the original hermaphroditic state and achieving perfect happiness.

"Fuck," we say, looking at each other.

The hermaphrodite craze consumes our globe. The creature is all over the TV: ecstasy delight splendor glory harmony.

We want to tear our hair out.

The other hermaphrodites are delivered to Earth in the second Emergency Escape Capsule. We begin to refer to these creatures as the Joined. The new ones appear on TV. Whenever a word like "loneliness" or "dissatisfaction" or "boredom" comes up, they offer only kind, puzzled smiles. The Joined describe their experience of the world as clean, bright, fresh, fragrant. Can this possibly be the same place where we live?

We happen to be watching—as we so often are—during a glitch. The middle-aged female astronaut, the same lady who'd run off into the woods, is on a show in her Joined form, talking relentlessly about joy, when a guy with crazy gray hair bursts onto the set and starts yelling, weeping, and gesticulating.

"Gertrude," he cries. "Gertrude."

The hermaphrodite looks with bemused benevolence at this silly skinny man.

"Dearest," he says.

"Excuse me," the hostess says. "We're going to take a short break for commercials but we'll be right back!"

When we return to the show a couple of minutes later, the old guy has disappeared, and the Joined is saying something about serenity, her bare breasts hanging above her belly.

The President announces that the new planet will be called Htrae. We soon realize how shortsighted his decision is when we hear the newscasters trying to pronounce it. In the past, this would have amused us, but a new anxiety has settled over our living room.

The United Nations, eager to preside over a world of contented citizens and to boost the lagging SpaceBus industry, launches a program to match every person on Earth with his/her corresponding being on Htrae. The head of the nascent agency swears that through his own blood, sweat, and tears he'll make sure everyone becomes Joined. Matches are based on six traits identified and tested by a fast-working group of doctors: (1) gender, (2) height, (3) birth date, (4) blood type, (5) shape of skull, (6) shape of intestines. If these six indicators are in place, the match is guaranteed. A team is sent to

Htrae to collect statistics, which are then input into a vast computerized database. With increasing frequency, people from Earth travel to Htrae and become Joined. "Twe am," they all say. On Earth, we celebrate for them.

So this means if they found a female on Htrae who was five feet ten inches tall, who was born on October 11 twenty-four years ago, who had Z+ blood, who had a little dimple in the skull above her ear, who had God knows what kind of intestines, then—

If they found a male on Htrae who was five feet five inches tall, who was born on February 9 twenty-three years ago, who had Y- blood, who had no irregularities in the skull, who—

"Yes," we say. "Then."

So we take our paperwork in. We do what we're told. We, too, have been lonely and disappointed. We, like everyone, wish for something slightly different and better. Like everyone, we hope. We wait.

And one day we get home from work to discover a single official letter in the mailbox. A match has been indisputably located! The letter informs us that the matched citizen is invited to catch a SpaceBus to Htrae tomorrow.

We gaze around the apartment, at our shabby couch and the small pile of unwashed dishes, at the seahorse lamp with the green shade and the bedspread that looks like it was stolen from a second-rate motel. One of us will be here, still watching the television, still wrapped in the dark blue blanket, still finding gingersnap crumbs between the cushions.

We begin to pack the suitcase. We disagree about what

should go in. The only thing we can agree on is that not much will be needed. Once you're Joined, nothing matters anymore, or so it seems. You wouldn't be able to fit into your old shirts and pants, obviously, and the Joined prefer nudity even when given the option of the fine new clothing being designed for their bodies. Their skin always looks radiant, so what good will cocoa butter cream do you? Halfway through, we resolve to forget about toothbrushes, shampoo, socks, books.

Tonight, since it's our last night, we decide to leave the living room and go walking along the river. Sure, there's garbage and empty beer bottles down there, but with a lifetime of rapture ahead, it's easy not to be bothered by such things. We carry the official letter with us.

We stop and sit on a cement barrier where the bank of the river should be. The moon is yellow and slender. We try to spot Htrae, but our eyes aren't good enough.

We sit there in silence.

No more nights when the tossing and turning of one keeps the other up. No more debates about whether Brussels sprouts should be steamed or fried. No more disagreements about the timer on the air conditioner. No more of those startling sneezes. No more weird smells. No more loud chewing, no more forgetting to clean up the honey when it explodes on the kitchen floor, no more slamming the closet door too early in the morning.

We sit there for a long time.

We use a method we learned in elementary school. We fold the letter in half and tear along the creases. We rip it again and again and again until it's in so many tiny pieces it's like it has vanished.

At home, you take a shower even though there's mildew. I sit on the toilet seat. The toenail clippers are nowhere to be found. A whitish towel dangles off the sink. A smear of toothpaste on the counter. A piece of dental floss hanging from the trash can. The shower curtain's red barbershop stripes move as you shampoo. When you knock the soap out of the shower and onto the floor, I pick it up. The bathroom fills with steam until we're just a couple of blobs in the mirror.

FLESH AND BLOOD

It began on Tuesday morning; my landlord had been in Florida over the long weekend, and when I glimpsed him schlubbing around in the backyard two stories down, I was stricken by the extreme redness of his skin. Florida! The place where old white men go to turn bloodred. I stepped away from the window. I'd been to Florida once, a big group of friends, a happy bright blur of a week, so long ago.

Showering, smoothing lotion onto my arms and legs, I enjoyed the healthy golden quality of my skin. In the mirror my face seemed almost to shimmer. I felt clean inside and out, my morning poop having arrived precisely on schedule, my immaculate stomach awaiting milk, granola, apple.

It was not that there was anything displeasing about

my life. Still youngish, still prettyish, a tiny tidy apartment, parents to visit and friends to complain to, a guy with whom I'd been on a series of lighthearted dates, a photography hobby and a hostessing job at a French restaurant where they deferred to me when it came to arranging the flowers, no great grief or heartbreak, a few moments of lonesomeness and meaninglessness here and there; it pleased me to think of myself as a person like any other.

Somehow I managed to stay in my own world all the way to the bus stop. It happens in big cities. But then, boarding the bus and inserting my pass, I saw the bus driver's arm and hand, his fingers tapping the wheel.

First there was the instinct to gag, but, ever polite, I tamped it down. Second there was the rational explanation: He's a veteran, how tragic, don't stare. Yet the soothing logic of that explanation faded as my gaze moved up his arm to his neck, his face.

I could see his muscles, his blood vessels, the stretchiness of his tendons, the bulge of his eyeballs, the color of his skull.

The other passengers trying to board the bus were getting restless, pushing a bit and clearing their throats. I turned around to give them a look of compassion and warning. The woman behind me was wearing a light brown raincoat; I perceived this raincoat as I turned; atop the raincoat, the woman's skinless head.

Gagging, I stumbled forward into the bus.

"Yaawlrite?" the bus driver said in some language I didn't recognize, his bloodred muscles contracting to reveal teeth that appeared uncannily white.

I grabbed a metal pole and clung to it. When I opened my eyes: rows upon rows of skinless faces, eyeballs bulging and mouths forming grimaces as they observed the little scene I was making.

"Wanna sit, sweetheart?" one of them said, standing. A man, probably, though it was hard to tell.

I shook my head and gripped the pole. I would never, ever sit among them. The idea was so horrifying, so absurd, that I half-giggled. The "man" shrugged and sat back down.

There was hope. That this would end once I got off the bus. That this bus was cursed or fucked or something. In honor of this hope, I averted my eyes.

"What's wrong, baby girl?" Sasha said, his grimace widening as he whirled past with a pair of wineglasses dangling from the sinewy complexity of his hand. I realized the grimace was their equivalent of a smile. "Table nine's killing me, just sent back a bottle of cab sauv, Bo's in quite a mood, shit the phone."

Frozen at the hostess stand, I gazed out over a scene from hell, well-dressed arrangements of tendon and muscle and bone sipping wine and poking at salads.

I watched the shiny white fat tremble on Bo's arms and neck as he yelled, "A*ru*gula!"

In the lavender-scented bathroom I puked—searingly aware of the bile as it passed upward through the caverns and passageways of my body—until there was nothing left, and then I wished I could puke some more.

There was a knock.

"Oh, pardon me." A civilized British accent contrasted

unbearably with the petite capillary-laced package that stepped graciously aside when I opened the door.

They sent me away kindly, solicitous words emerging from their hideous mouths, advice to drink ginger tea and watch romantic comedies; I'd always been well-liked. As they spoke, I tried to focus on the clean, empty space above their heads. It was a relief to step outside.

Yet the streets offered no respite.

A squirrel without skin or fur or bushy tail, demonic; a dog stalking down the sidewalk like a creature from a nightmare, all its organs revealed.

Upon passing a playground, I had to hold my face in my hands for some minutes. Skipping and hopping, pumping on swings and hanging from bars, unaware of the appalling interplay of their tissues and blood vessels. I witnessed an ice cream sandwich descending a child's gullet.

I attempted to take shelter in the pure white dressing room of a clothing store, but pulling a shirt over my head it occurred to me that probably one of them had tried on this selfsame shirt, had yanked it over the repulsive intricacy of the face, the gut.

On the bus, an infant drowsed in its mother's revolting arms; the infant slightly less terrible than everybody else, as one is accustomed to newborns looking bloody, almost transparent, when they emerge.

At home there truly was respite. I stood in front of the mirror, naked, breathing deeply, calmer with each second I spent gazing at a normal human being. It wasn't that it was my body (sure, I appreciated the familiarity, the undeniable appeal of the breasts and nipples), but just that it was a body. With skin.

I cried for joy. Up until then I'd never believed people could cry for joy.

Then I touched myself and soon cried out for joy, bending over the dresser as I lost myself to it.

I closed my curtains. I got out all my glossy photography books, models and famous people, and enjoyed them, their skin and facial features and the unity of their bodies.

Did I think it would pass?

I must have believed it would.

Calling in to take a week off work; scuttling out to the corner store to buy provisions (pickles, bread, milk, canned peaches, peanut butter, spaghetti, tomato sauce), barely enduring the sight of the cashier's ligaments as he handled the groceries; sending friends lilting, dodgy texts in response to their phone calls—nobody could actually plan to live this way.

Then Mom called to say they were making the two-hour drive down to the city this weekend, wanted to whisk me away to a nearby beach for the afternoon. This was quite normal, happened every few weeks in the summertime, and was one of my life's little delights; unlike most people, I really couldn't think of anything fraught to say about my parents.

I asked Mom not to make the drive this weekend, maybe next weekend or the following, but I went about it the wrong way, overly casual in a way that struck her as not casual at all. She became instantly suspicious and worried, more insistent than ever about visiting.

"Okay," I was finally forced to whimper, "okay, okay."

It would be best not to go to the beach. Too much skin, or lack thereof. Staying in the city would be better. Brunch, followed by some kind of passive activity that didn't involve the removal of any layers of clothing. How about a dark movie theater? But I knew my parents would never agree to watch a movie when they could be spending time with me. *We can go to the movies any old day!* they'd say jovially, showering me with love.

I thought hard about the ideal location for brunch. A crowded diner might be good—plenty of distractions—but could I stand a roomful of noisily eating bodies? I could make brunch at home, which would be simplest, but there were numerous problems with that—firstly, that I refused to buy food anywhere except the corner store; secondly, that being alone with my parents' skinless bodies sounded devastating; thirdly, that the apartment was my one respite.

Ultimately I decided on a picnic in the park. Other people, but not too many. And Mom would enjoy putting the picnic together. Indeed, when I called her back to suggest this, I could hear the muscles of her mouth pulling back into a smile. The fact that I could *hear* this sound did not bode well.

I did—of course I did—entertain the hope that my parents wouldn't appear skinless to me.

On Saturday, there was a fraction of an instant of optimism when I opened the front door of my building, a promising glimpse of Mom's jeans and Dad's baseball cap.

Gently, I refused to let them come upstairs into the apartment, raving about the beauty of the day and how eager I was to get to the park. My mother—my dear, veiny, bony mother—had packed a splendid picnic, and we sat on an actual red-and-white checkered tablecloth by the lake. Hard-boiled eggs, grapes, seltzer, et cetera. My parents, birdwatchers, talked about the swans and the ducks and the red-winged blackbirds and even thought they glimpsed a heron; birds, as you can imagine, as elaborate and disconcerting as human hands.

Dad! Why did he have to wear those damn khaki shorts?

It bothered Mom that I wouldn't eat the tuna fish salad sandwich she'd made sans mayonnaise especially for me. *Sans mayonnaise,* she kept repeating that, and passing me clumps of grapes gripped in the web of her finger bones. Furtively, I placed the grapes in the grass behind me. I tried to focus solely on my parents' irises, which were less dramatically affected than everything else.

But it was exhausting, and soon enough I couldn't help but shut my eyes, and lie down on the picnic blanket, and pretend to sleep. Resting there with my eyes closed, listening to my parents' voices, I could almost believe they weren't a pair of capillary-encrusted skeletons. When they were sure I was asleep, they talked about me. Nothing they said offended me. They were sad I didn't have someone to love, they hoped I wasn't dissatisfied with my life, they were proud of what a sensible and self-sufficient person I'd become. When I "woke up" they said they'd enjoyed watching over my sleep, just like when I was a baby. This comment would have made me feel cozy if it hadn't been emerging from my father's uncanny mouth.

It took a lot out of me to muzzle my scream when Mom removed her sweatshirt, her flowered T-shirt lifting for an instant to reveal her midsection.

It was bad enough to see strangers and acquaintances this way. But to see your own parents. To be forced to acknowledge the architecture of their bodies, the chaos of their blood vessels, the humility of their skulls. To know that this vulnerability was the place from which you arose.

After that I was careful to avoid looking at them at all. I controlled the shiver of disgust I felt when Mom hugged me good-bye; when Dad hugged me good-bye, the disgust transformed suddenly to pity, which was, alarmingly, far worse. I implored them not to come upstairs, I'd had people over last night, the kitchen was a disaster, I was ashamed.

Upstairs, alone in my very clean, quiet kitchen, I washed my hands and arms and neck and face, trying to scrub off every place where they'd touched me. Then I ran to the bathroom and stood under the shower and cried at the delicacy of my parents. Then I went to stand in front of the mirror and enjoy my skin. But I got distracted by the silence of my apartment. It had become the most silent place in the world.

There was that guy. No big deal, but we'd been on six or seven dates. It wasn't as though I thought he was the one, but our dates had been long and rambling and funny and already it had become a little bit sad when we had to part ways after an epic twelve-hour stretch spent in each other's company. So he'd been calling and emailing left and right this whole time and I'd been dodging him with brief, hopefully witty one-liners.

Yet now here he is outside my door with a pair of gerbera daisies and a blue bicycle and a face of raw bone and muscle.

"Fuck you," he says, "here I am."

I'd laugh if I weren't working so hard to not look at him.

"Can I bring my bike in," he states.

I swing the door all the way open to let him pass. Unfortunately, he's wearing shorts and flip-flops. I watch the tendons work as he walks the bike down the short hall. Actually this angle—the back of the leg, the heel—isn't so bad.

The skinless cock looks strange, pale, like something from outer space. The balls are gooey and more fragile than anything. As it hardens and grows, the cock becomes even creepier, yet somehow more defenseless, too. I'm shocked to find myself going a little bit wet, but then he shoves his eerie lips at mine.

I'm seeing parts of the human body I've never seen, lungs and intestines, liver and ribs, bizarre constructions.

Yet I accept him. I twist my neck, I shut my eyes. Inside it feels the same as ever; good, present. The lack of skin doesn't make a difference. I love it terribly much. I don't dare open my eyes.

But then, getting close, unable to keep them shut at a time like this (I know I should simply focus on his irises, his merciful dark brown irises), I look down upon two bodies, a pulsing beating body of linked organs versus a smooth clean body enwrapped in skin. I reach to pull him closer, harder, better—and as my hand goes out and around to grab his neck, I catch a glimpse of my fingers, the complicated muscles and tendons and bones, my hand a weird blood-colored bird.

WHEN THE TSUNAMI CAME

When the tsunami came, we—my husband and I—were not among the good. We were in the street alongside all the neighbors who had for so many years remained strangers to us. The wave, it was thirty feet high, straight from Coney Island, the roller coaster in pieces.

It was a bright day in March.

The wave contained many things that might be listed here for poetic effect, things of the teacup-and-crib variety, but it did not look marvelous to us. It looked like garbage. The newspaper didn't lie: *You could measure the wave's advance by the clouds of dust created by collapsing buildings.*

There was that elderly couple from Apartment IB. Campbell was their last name, or Winslow. I'd sometimes worried they could hear us when we had sex. They didn't look rich but they did have a Jaguar, and early on Saturday mornings while I was outside waiting for the Laundromat to open, they'd walk slowly past on the way to their Jaguar. They wore nice clothes, lavender and brown, and seemed to be going somewhere halfway fun and halfway not, like the cemetery followed by the pancake house. "That Laundromat won't open till after eight," the Mrs. once warned me. Old people: they want things to work out. "You should go to the Laundromat down the street," she insisted. "Thank you," I said, politely; I'd always believed myself to be kinder than average. "Thank you," I repeated, filled with gratitude, though of course I stayed right where I was. I've now shared with you everything I knew about the inhabitants of Apartment IB.

It's impossible to know, until you're in a situation, whether you're good or bad. *I saw the ugly side of people, and then I saw the good side. Some people only thought of themselves. They were shoving old people out of the way.*

Yet think of the punishment: for the rest of your life, you're not worthy of a glass of water, even though you know the young are right to save themselves.

GAME

She's been sucking on violet candies all day and now her mouth is bleeding. These candies have sharp edges and taste like perfume. Only she and spinsters from the nineteenth century could be capable of enjoying such candies. They have a game where she forces him to eat violet candies unless he's able to recall whatever obscure fact about which she is quizzing him—her mother's middle

"We'll have fun, won't we?"

"It wasn't where you said it was."

name, for instance, or her brother's birthday. Rose hips grow alongside the road, so large they look cancerous. Everything is oversize, overgrown. They're in a car but it feels as though they are bicycling down the road. All these dreamy, nightmarish plants closing in on them, reaching out onto the pavement. Rose hips, and poison ivy, honeysuckle, sea grass. He drives slow. Wind swirls inside and outside the car. She doesn't need to tell him that her mouth is bleeding. He already knows this, just as he knows everything about her. They have a game where she asks him: Can you guess what I'm feeling?

Can you guess what I'm feeling? she says with her bloody mouth. They have been sad quite recently, so nobody should begrudge them their current happiness. They were married in a year that's a multiple of ten, so it will always be easy to

"We'll say it was a golden time of day."

"I'm not bored."

"You didn't find my coat?"

remember the next important anniversary. Seventy-five years is in the realm of possibility. She enjoys this fact, and places another violet candy on her tongue.

"Kind of gloomy."

At the far desolate end of the beach, an insect lands on her nipple. It's some kind of greenish fly, and she allows it to stay there, moving its torso swiftly up and down, until he becomes jealous of it and leaves his book splayed open on the sand. She feels very tenderly toward the fly as it flies away. This tenderness extends to him and also to the seagulls, and to the old naked people they passed by. They lie on their sides, his stomach against her back. Whenever a tourist wanders by with a camera they disconnect, separate, loll innocently on their respective towels. This becomes a sort of game. The joy is almost unpleasant because even in the midst of it you are

"If only we could remember the date!"

"The broccoli was overcooked."

"The deviled eggs were embarrassing."

"I'm not sure."

"You mean you aren't feeling radiant?"

"Still *snowing?*"

"You don't remember what I said?"

already starting to dread the moment when you will no longer be in the midst of it. Above, enormous black birds hover over the ocean, awaiting fish or something. Below, they continue what they have begun. Interrupted seven times, he becomes desperate. *Are those vultures?* she says at the exact moment. Distracted, he never hears her question, and for the rest of time it will remain unanswered. Meanwhile, he puts his finger up inside her. *You want to know the difference between you and him?* she says, worn out and warm. Her lips already sunburned and swollen. *With him I said Oh God and with you I say Oh fuck.* This fact delights him and suddenly he wants to play Frisbee with her. But they have no Frisbee, or if they do she's hidden it at the bottom of the bag and lied to him. *How about this,* she says, *I'll give you a quiz.* He says: *Your mouth is still bloody,*

"Wait a sec, I'm not ready yet."

"I had a nightmare I think."

"Do you think they're happy?"

"Yeah, chamomile."
"Did you?"
"It'll be good."

isn't it. She says: *Our marriage is most like: (a) a ball of glass, (b) a ball of twigs, (c) a ball of seaweed, (d) a ball of concrete, or (e) all of the above.* Something dark plops into the ocean. They both see it. It's probably a bird, or maybe something else. They wait for it to reemerge but it never does. So maybe it was something that had never been alive, such as a rock or a transistor radio, or maybe it was something that had gone into the ocean and died there. Inside his hand, she crosses her fingers, wondering if this gesture maintains its protective power when performed within the context of a handhold. *What am I feeling?* He says: *When the Muslims came to Spain they converted cathedrals into mosques. They took the tiles that had been used to render the Virgin Mary and reworked them into mosaics of flowers. You feel like the Virgin Mary transformed into flowers.* This is beautiful but not quite accurate.

"Did you put it on the list?"

"I'm exhausted. Is there any food left?"

"No more wine?"

"Hurry up."

"The garbage stinks again already."

"I still can't hear you."

"My eyes are hurting."

"Don't we have any medicine?"

Its lack of accuracy exhausts
her, and she falls asleep. When
she wakes up seventeen minutes
later, she looks different. The
towel has left strange patterns
on her skin. Her chin is vaguer
and less youthful than before.
He doesn't enjoy looking at her
but can't stop staring. *What?* she
says. *What?*
Let's play a game, she says. *Stand up.*
She stands in front of him.
She's wearing nothing
but sunglasses and a strand of
seaweed. From this angle he
can't perceive the horrific
changes in her face. He's drowsy
and not in the mood for
another game and wants to
remain at this pleasing angle
but he rises out of guilt for the
moment when he found her
appearance repulsive. *Pretend I'm
vanishing,* she says. Slowly she
walks backward toward the
ocean. *Pretend I'm about to disappear into the waves and you'll never
see me again.* She raises her arms
and holds them straight out in

"It's getting late."
"Your jeans stink."

"You didn't take care of
that?"

"The timing is off."
"Pass those over here?"

"I'm so sick of winter."

"I didn't sleep well."

"Thank you."
"Why don't you brush
your teeth first?"
"I can't believe you're not
cold."

"It'll be a nice enough
day."
"The texture's all
wrong."

front of her, hands limp. *Pretend you have one chance to save me before I go into the sea forever.* He suggests that she drink some water. *Come on, imagine it!* He says she looks dehydrated. He unzips the backpack and pulls out an apple. He asks if her mouth is still bleeding. *I'm serious,* she says. *I'm about to vanish into the ocean and if you don't come and get me then you'll never, ever see me again.* She steps backward, very slowly. He drops the apple on the towel and moves toward her. As he approaches she turns and begins to run. She runs up and down, all in circles, and he follows, his penis waggling, but, incredibly, she manages to stay just out of his grasp. *Catch me!* she yells. *Catch me or I'll disappear forever!* She sprints toward the waves. He realizes then that he has become involved in a game whose rules are innumerable, obscure, opaque. He follows her at full speed, grabs at the air behind her. She crosses the

"What was that?"

"You have to sign this."
"I'll be back as soon as I can, okay?"
"I'll go to the bank."

"You used to love this show."
"I just thought you might forget."
"We ran out of bread?"
"I didn't think it would be like this."
"Doesn't this color make me look ill?"
"The refrigerator is broken."
"Did you hear that noise?"
"You know I prefer almond."
"No, at seven."
"How was it?"
"They didn't have the brand you like."
"You mean you lost the keys?"

threshold of the ocean. Water splashes up high. She runs into a wave. On shore, he falls to his knees.

On the beach, an orange rolls and rolls in the waves. It looks too orange against the sand. It keeps rolling back and forth in a perfect line as though it has always been right there and will always be right there. *Do you think the brine preserves the orange?* she says.

"My stomach hurts."
"It's too bright for me."
"I hope you don't mind oatmeal."
"Do you remember that monkey?"
"The toilet's still running."
"It might rain."
"Fine, I'll do it."
"They aren't any better than you."
"I couldn't find it."
"Shut the window before you go, okay?"

ONE OF US WILL BE HAPPY;
IT'S JUST A MATTER OF WHICH ONE

Once upon a time and for all time, a Queen and King sat on twin thrones. They were beloved, this Queen and King, for she was famous across the land as a wife who valued above all else the happiness of her husband and he was famous across the land as a husband who valued above all else the happiness of his wife. A never-ending line of their devoted subjects wound through the long hallways of the castle and out onto the high road. These subjects stepped confidently into the throne room, their simple shoes softly slapping the marble floors, which were checkered like a chessboard. There was nothing servile about the behavior of the subjects; they were treated with dignity and behaved with dignity.

The subjects would place before the Queen and King the riches of their fields and streams, their forests and barns.

Sunflowers would pile up, and sheaves of wheat, and the skinned bodies of small mammals. Great baskets of eggs and wooden boxes filled with honeycombs. Heaps of wool and heaps of silver fish; piles of pumpkins and piles of stones. At times these riches were accompanied by or replaced with devastating news: a fire, a flood, a drought, a debt. The lips of the Queen and the lips of the King would rise and sink accordingly, up into smiles of bounty, down into frowns of grief. The subjects well knew that joy shared is joy doubled, sorrow shared is sorrow halved, et cetera.

And thus life was good and bad, abundant and lean, ecstatic and tragic, blessed and cursed, all at once, on and on, forever and ever, until the end of time.

Sometimes young women would arrive, in pairs or in a flock; these girls danced upon the chessboard, singing folk songs at once strange and familiar, like something heard in the womb. The King did not know if it was the Queen who arranged these performances for him, or if some castle ringmaster called for the girls. They danced, flinging their scarves into the air; how exquisite the varying shades of their skin, how luminous their eyes and calves.

Yes, the King was acutely aware of them, of the heat between his legs as they threw themselves across the cool marble. And the Queen, too, was acutely aware of them, of the ways in which the shapes of their bodies aped and diverged from the shape of hers.

Did she call for them in order to bring pleasure to the King, or to taunt him, or to tempt him? The Queen herself did not know the answer to this question; indeed, had a different answer to it at each hour of the day.

Someday the King would step down from his throne, would go to one of these young women, would vanish with her down a hallway, would return to his throne sometime later, a changed man or an unchanged man. Someday the Queen would watch the King step down from his throne and go to one of the girls and take this girl to a tower in the far reaches of the castle, where he would presumably drag his finger from the center of her forehead downward, would release a cry that arced over the castle and down to the throne room where the Queen sat, listening. And when the King returned to his throne, she would love him the exact same amount as before, or would love him slightly more, or would love him quite a bit less. It was possible that when he reached for her (his palm still sweaty with another woman's sweat), his hand would feel like a knife. Or perhaps when he reached for her, his hand would feel as exuberant as fire, and the Queen would touch the joy.

Or perhaps the King would never act; perhaps that heat between his legs would cool and shrivel. Perhaps the Queen would live out all the days of her life luxuriating in the King's unmarred devotion, and would scarcely notice the moment when death arrived for her amid the blinding brightness of that devotion, which all along had kept her as close to paradise as a human woman could ever hope to dwell: safe, warm, calm.

Or perhaps the Queen would come to see herself as a jail warden, an impossibly heavy ring of keys slung around her waist, guarding the smallest, most absurd cell in the universe: a tiny barred box just big enough for an old man's penis.

The Queen and King sat on their twin thrones while the parade of subjects poured its momentary riches, its fruits, its girls, onto the chessboard before them. Once in a blue moon, you might be lucky enough to overhear him whispering to her or her whispering to him.

"One of us will be sad," he or she would say, "it's just a matter of which one."

And you might catch the other replying: "One of us will be happy; it's just a matter of which one."

THINGS WE DO

1.

I had this joke with someone I used to love. We'd say to each other: Saying I love you, that's *our* thing, our special thing, just for the two of us. Whatever becomes of us, you can't ever say that to anyone else. Or: Having sex, that's *our* thing, our special thing, you better never do that with anyone else, not even if we split up. You can do other things with them, of course, you can do anything you want with anyone you want at any time under the sun, but never that, because that's *our* thing.

Later, I tried to reinvigorate this joke with someone I loved far more: Going to the bar, drinking gin & tonics, getting drunk and having lots to talk about, that's *our* thing. Marriage, that's *our* thing, wherever you go and whatever you do and whoever you meet, remember that. But, dismayingly, the joke was no longer hilarious; now when I said it I sounded like I meant it.

2.

Removed, the wedding ring and the engagement ring lie obediently together upon the ledge. That's the thing about objects, they're so obedient, and it's a goddamn relief if you ask me. You put them there upon the ledge and there they shall stay until someone or something comes along.

3.

We shouldn't keep drinking $3 gin & tonics, but it takes more imagination than we've got to stop doing so, plus the sunsetting light is the color of booze and outside in the yard behind the bar the wall of ivy quivers like something from a lovelier place.

4.

Recently I've developed an addiction to the word *FEROCIOUS*—I've had other addictions at other times, such as *LULLABY, JUBILANT, HOWEVER*—and have started using it too much, mainly in my head but also out loud, using it to say things like "I had to be ferocious to figure out how to put that Ikea bookshelf together; I had to be especially ferocious with the top part."

5.

Our friends compliment the plants we have in our apartment. They say, "Wow, you have a lot of nice little plants."

And I say, "Thank you, yes, we went to the plant nursery and that's where we got those plants. The plant nursery on Euclid Avenue, if you were wondering."

But their eyes have already glazed over.

And you—you yawned the whole time we were selecting our plants!

6.

The only emperor is the emperor of ice cream.

Naked, bestial, I squatted.

I have this idea that lines recalled from poems we read in English class might help. Although that second line was purely your idea—inspired by the way I was crouching on our darkly gleaming wooden floor at three in the morning. Your delivery of such an apt line, your flawless read of the situation—that's the sort of thing that gives me hope. It also gives me hope when we put on the music and dance around our apartment.

I won't deny it: I'm a sucker for hope these days.

7.

I could get pregnant, you know, from all this makeup sex we're always having.

What?

I could get pregnant from all this messing around.

What?

Maybe you should come up here from down there.

What?

Maybe we could talk. Maybe you could hear me better.

You won't get pregnant.

8.

I have this idea that I'm not going to write any untrue things anymore. I'm only going to write things that are true, true, true.

The Guy Who Yawned at the Plant Nursery says: "You've never written a word of fiction in your life."

9.

Say I am pregnant. How do you think it feels about all this poison?

$3 gin & tonic, lime on lips, meditating on the word *tonic*.

Surely to my great-grandmother that meant something different, something with herbs that would fix all sorts of problems.

10.

The Guy Who Calls Me Baby doesn't come out very often, but when he does, I feel shy around him, like a new bride.

He seems like the kind of guy with whom the metaphor of a boxing ring would resonate. So to please him I say: "We're like boxers in a boxing ring."

And he says (maybe to please me, who knows): "Yeah, baby, that's *just* it."

11.

In second grade we made leprechaun traps for St. Patrick's Day. We placed those little golden balls they use to decorate cakes inside our traps and left the traps on our desks. The next morning all the golden balls were gone but no one had caught a leprechaun. I can't remember what the purpose of this lesson was, Ms. Kroll, but I remember the witchy sound of your long fingernail scratching your scalp. It was exciting to make the traps and disappointing to find them empty, but overall it was a time of belief.

"Look!" I choose to say now, to The Guy Who Just Bought Another Round, "there's a leprechaun scaling the wall of ivy!

"Oh bummer," I say, "sorry, you missed it."

12.

He says, "I desire you." He means, "Every night I dream of other women."

She says, "I desire you." She means, "I want to get accidentally pregnant."

13.

Maybe thirteen should be left blank, like those buildings with no thirteenth floor. That's another thing, I get more superstitious by the year. In a few decades I'll be wearing garlic around my neck.

14.

My husband is having trouble sleeping. I think he's thinking about sex.

He tells me that when he does finally manage to sleep, he dreams that everyone in his family hates him except for his one weird cousin.

15.

I crouch on the bed, massaging The Guy Who Thinks I Don't Know How to Use the Word *Renovate* Properly. Doing this reminds me of working with clay, slowly squeezing until something grows from nothing. Not that I've ever worked with clay. Not that I've ever made a bowl that could hold anything.

16.

You may say: "We really ought to *renovate* the bathroom." You may not say: "We need to *renovate* our thinking about this problem."

17.

In a hotel room in Cincinnati, someone's ninety-year-old grandmother is falling in the bathtub and snapping three small ribs.

In Pakistan the waters that have already risen are rising more. I'm sorry, but it's pretty much just the babies I think of. I'm only interested in statistics about how many infants have drowned. As soon as I know that, then I'll be able to properly mourn.

18.

So many bombs shattering across the globe, yet it was private grief that kept them up at night.

19.

He said: "Please don't put things in third person past tense. Just because it's third person past tense doesn't mean it's a story. It's not as though third person past tense will protect you."

She said: "He said, *Please don't put things in third person past tense,* and then she said, *He said please don't put things in third person past tense.*"

20.

I've thrown up three times since I've known him:

(I) The night before he proposed, in Guatemala, black bean soup/Montezuma's revenge.

(2) The night before the miscarriage and the apartment closing, which happened, impossibly, to fall on the same day. The baby fell into a toilet designed by a designer to conserve water. He said: "If by 'baby' you mean 'minuscule bundle of cells,' then I'll let the above sentence slide."

(3) Last week, for no reason at all, after eating Thai Iced Tea Ice Cream, which is quite an orange color if I do say so myself. Of course I was thinking about the invisible baby the whole time, and the way it would be three months old by now, and the way my grief exceeded his by so much, and the way I don't want to be filled with vitriol, a word thank God I learned when I was studying for a standardized test. God it was so hot the night of the Thai Iced Tea Ice Cream Sickness, and my beloved was so good to me that night, so exceedingly patient.

21.

Our friends admire our marriage and ask us for advice.

When I think about the phrase "hitch our wagons" it almost makes me cry because it is so beautiful, so accurate, so beautiful.

22.

Once something I wrote made the judge of a contest indignant. He wrote, "This is something that this woman should share with her husband alone, if with anyone, and probably not even with him."

23.

He's always called me his "Little Try-er." He says: "You are always try, try, trying to make things good." This is both a compliment and an insult.

24.

Lightbulbs make me feel peaceful these days, as do water glasses.

Wikipedia makes me feel safe and newspapers make me feel guilty.

Facebook makes me want to change my life and Twitter makes me want to stay the way I am.

25.

The person with whom I used to have the joke about never saying *I love you* to anyone else recently told me: "You would have been happy no matter who you married. You always loved everyone. I mean that as a compliment."

We had not seen each other for many years. We were walking the hills of San Francisco that day and truly everything seemed possible.

26.

The Guy Who Has Urges Impossible to Satisfy comes up to the bar and grabs my ass. He's very predictable but that doesn't mean he doesn't scare me.

At night, together, in bed, sleepless, we're more in the same boat than we've been in a long time.

Boat, that's good too, a helpful image. But when I try to picture it what I see is fog, a wooden boat with old oars, the desperate expressions on our faces.

27.

"I'm a monster, I'm a monster, I'm a monster, I'm a monster," he says four times in a row, just like that, and I can't tell if he's joking or serious.

28.

He says, "You are like, you are like, you are like a glass of cold water that I drink from every morning."

He's always coming up with these extremely useful metaphors. He's the best decision I ever made.

He says, "Why are you always saying that language falls short?"

29.

On nights when I can't sleep I dream that our apartment is way larger than I ever realized. It has nooks and crannies and lofts I never knew about. In fact, there is a section of our apartment where an entire forest could be planted!

30.

I had this plan that I would be happier this year than ever before. That day by day, twig by twig, I would construct my inner nest, and meanwhile my skin would be better than ever and my patience would be infinite and I'd be able to talk easily with strangers, and maybe even would finally learn how to whistle, and wouldn't be scared of driving.

If only that famous person hadn't written me to say: *Happiness in marriage is an illusion.* Jesus Christ, who puts that kind of thing in an email?

31.

When he pointed at me and shouted, "You!" I couldn't tell if I was being singled out for love or scorn.

32.

"All I want is X," he says. "That's all. Just X."

"X," I say. "Jesus Christ."

"Please," he says, "stop calling me that."

I wonder if it's a technical thing, hitching your wagons, something involving rope and a metal loop, or if it's merely a turn of phrase.

You've just got to disconnect your happiness from my happiness, okay? Okay?

33.

What's with this feeling of dread? Two weeks ago I wrote an email to an old friend proclaiming my transcendent happiness, or at least the promise of it.

Seven fireflies, a pink evening, whatever, there was cause for confidence, and there still is, hello, it's not as though we're doomed.

34.

We turn the air conditioner off.

We turn the air conditioner on.

We close the door.

We open the door.

We think of our parents and their deaths.

We think of our children and their births.

It is hot yet I need hot milk. I understand that it's disgusting to drink milk intended for the young of a different species, yet I can never get enough of it.

35.

"You're being so nice to me right now," The Girl with the Hot Milk says. "Thank you."

"No, thank YOU," The Guy Standing by the Air Conditioner says.

"Oh," she says, "oh, I hope we're always this nice to each other."

36.

In the grocery store I see a woman with an infant. She reminds me of me. She's even got a zit where I've got a zit. When I approach her, she smiles.

"Hey there," she says.

Why am I not surprised to see milk, limes, a jar of golden balls in her cart?

"What's your baby's name?" I say, realizing as I say it that my voice sounds ferocious, as though it's been ages since I used it in polite company.

But the young woman just winks at me. "You know what," she says, "I haven't even given her a name yet."

R

This one day my sister and I were walking in the park when something happened. We saw or felt or heard or smelled or sensed something we'd never seen or felt or heard or smelled or sensed before. Due to our inexperience with this kind of experience, we had no vocabulary for it, though we tried.

"Soft," my sister said.

"Powerful," I suggested.

"Perfume-y," my sister attempted.

"Redolent of dirt," I embellished.

"What does 'redolent' mean?"

She was a less devoted student of the Internet, and thus still ignorant.

The park stretched before us and behind us. From this

vantage, I could hardly believe in the city that smushed up against its concrete borders. The park's groves had been planted with precision, yet at this time of year the variety in the leaves' shades of orange and pink lent them a satisfying randomness.

In any case, this thing my sister and I encountered in the park changed the park. The park was always utterly still, its gleaming lawns green and unmoving, its groves brilliant and still, its ponds still and green with algae, clouds of purple asters hovering still and silent. Sure, there were bits of movement here and there—a white swan stroking its way through the black water, or a squirrel with a singed tail moving ratlike toward an overflowing garbage bin. A handful of birds taking flight from a chokecherry bush; an abandoned eighth-of-a-sandwich moving wondrously on the backs of a thousand cooperative ants. But other than these few gestures provided by the innocently exuberant creatures of the park, who seemed to exist in complete ignorance of the raging city beyond, there was never any movement in the park. People, yes, of course; dogs, yes; a hired dog-walker with a herd of pure breeds; packs of children. Beyond these living beings, though, nothing in the park had ever moved or been moved. We had always cherished this stillness.

Until the moment in question. At which time everything in the park moved at once, in the same sequence of swirls and sways. Every blade of grass; every leaf; every twig; every aster; every discarded candy wrapper. For as far as our eyes could see, every single thing pressed toward our faces, and then away from our faces, and then to our right, and then to our left, again and again in repeating patterns, right, forward, leftish, backward, left, rightish, et cetera.

It was midday on a Wednesday (we were ungainfully employed as nighttime dancers) and the park was empty; no one else to witness this odd phenomenon, or to accuse us of insanity. We were partly terrified by the absence of others and partly grateful for it. I reached out for my sister's hand and/or she reached out for mine. We stood, absorbing this thing and searching for words.

"Pretty," she said.

"Disconcerting," I said.

This thing—you could feel it all over your skin.

"Fresh," she said. "Nice."

"Creepy," I proposed. "Aggressive."

I looked at my sister and she looked at me. We were identical twins; I emerged into the world six minutes before she did. I observed that this thing was capable of lifting her hair (identical to my hair—originally dullish brown but now long, coppery, curly with hair extensions), twisting and tugging and twining it around her arms and neck, around my arms and neck. It's amazing what synthetic hair will do for one's beauty; we are not *very* pretty but with our hair we give the impression of very pretty, which is far more important. Anyhow, the effect this thing had on our hair was quite an appealing one.

I observed that my sister's squinty eyes squinted even further against the force of this thing that was moving the park, so I knew my squinty eyes were squinting too.

"Goldeny," Roo offered.

"Colorless," I countered. "Invisible."

Back in our room we got on the Internet to search. Roo sat on my lap. She weighed three pounds less than I did, which gave her the right. I told her what to type and she typed. *Something that causes movement in the park,* which yielded only information about movies screened in the park in the summertime.

"I wish we'd gone to those," I said. We were always missing out on things.

Roo ignored me and kept typing. She typed her words: *Soft, Goldeny, Perfume-y, Nice, Pretty,* et cetera, which yielded, obviously, nothing relevant. Then she tried mine, misremembering "Redolent" as *Redundant. Colorless,* she tried. *Creepy.* Again, nothing. I shifted my knees because my legs were falling asleep, which made Roo slip off my lap and gash her head against the corner of the metal table.

I felt terrible.

"No big deal," Roo said calmly.

"Oh god," I said, looking at the blood, "oh god."

"Just keep searching!" Roo ordered. "It's fine. I'm fine."

I searched distractedly while listening to her rustling around in our bathroom, dabbing blood with toilet paper, hunting for Band-Aids in our nasty, chaotic drawers. I knew what she was doing as well as if I was in there with her. Pawing through rubber bands and scrunchies and hairpins sticky with spilled hair spray and old fluoride rinse. Mildew green between the pink tiles under her bare feet. The bowl of the toilet stained a permanent pale brown. The smell of a sour bathmat and cigar smoke from downstairs.

Halfheartedly, sick at heart to think of Roo finding only

dismembered Band-Aids in those drawers, I typed *trees swaying*, which got us where we needed to go.

Roo emerged with a bejeweled butterfly Band-Aid on her forehead, a Band-Aid designed for the little girls we'd once been in this very room; a Band-Aid that would go over extremely well tonight because in order to disguise the Band-Aid on the forehead we'd have to place a matching Band-Aid on each nipple.

I read: "The perceptible natural movement of the air, especially in the form of a current of air blowing from a particular direction."

"Yes! Yes!" Roo said, excited, jumping on the bed, throwing a pillow. "Exactly!"

"*Wind*," I announced.

The next morning (or rather, the next noon, since we were not allowed to come down to breakfast until we'd spent exactly nine hours in our room, for *Sleep is essential to beauty*; we were supposed to sleep precisely eight hours every night, plus a half-hour to put ourselves down and a half-hour to wake ourselves up, rules indifferent to our restlessness, our desire to go out into the ever-brightening day that we could sense on the other side of our miserly window), Mrs. Penelope was quite distressed to learn what we had encountered in the park. She threw the spatula across the room, where it left an eggy smear on the wall.

"For crying out loud," she said. She was an erratic, moody woman who vacillated between playing the role of tender mother and fierce madame. We were unsure which version we preferred. On days when she resembled a mother she seemed to weigh ten pounds more than she did on the madame days. Today was a madame day. We could tell by her slimming all-black outfit and the faux emeralds in her earlobes, and by the undercooked eggs and burnt toast. Mrs. Penelope the Mother would never make such mistakes. We were the only girls at the table, the last breakfast shift. The novelty of the butterfly Band-Aids had meant that Roo was tied up till nearly 3 a.m., and since we never left the place except together, I had to wait shivering in sequins on the busted couch in the back room, a spring screwing itself into my thigh as I tried and failed to recall the series of sensations created on the skin by the thing we'd encountered in the park.

Since all the other girls had been fed, there was no one to witness the things Mrs. Penelope the Lady said to me and especially to Roo about first of all making up such lies about wind in the park when wind had obviously not been seen or felt or anything in the two decades since the city got climate-controlled, and where the hell would such a wind come from, where would a lovely little wind like the one we described arise from in a region that was covered in concrete, for crying out loud, now get, time for your constitutional, and she was ranting us right out the door, and as we passed the enormous jug we deposited into it as usual everything we'd made last night, because the front door wouldn't open until money was inserted. The sight of our coins and bills shut her up and joyfully she squirted us with expensive perfume as we stumbled down the concrete steps onto the narrow strip of sidewalk alongside the six-lane street.

We walked thirteen blocks to get to the park. We had

heard rumors from other, less coveted girls that in the morning, when the sun was coming up, all the cars in the streets looked sleek and beautiful, but by the time we were released into the day the light had become flat and dull and the cars just looked gray to us.

Yet now we had something more than cars on our minds. We walked along silently, thinking the same thoughts. We did not linger outside the bodega as we usually did, gazing at the dusty rows of candy and packaged doughnuts. Even the dark, dank, concealing clothing we had to wear to the park—wool skirts that went down to our ankles above heavy, practical shoes and shirts that buttoned up to our necks beneath navy blue sweaters—did not seem quite as oppressive as usual.

Again, there was *wind* in the park.

It rose up when we reached the center of the lawn, just as it had yesterday. Again the park was abandoned and again we alone stood in the middle of the movement, our synthetic hair swirling around us. I understood now that wind was due to an interplay of hot and cold air.

From whence did it rise? I stretched my mind out across all the repetitive blocks of the city, stretched my mind to the outermost edge of my memory, blocks and blocks of gray buildings, gray streets, gray cars. That landscape, and the almost unbearably green landscape of the park, were the only landscapes I knew. Where could hot and cold meet and interact here? Nothing fresh arose from those temperate city blocks with their bags of trash piled high.

Yet this wind, this so-called wind, was as fresh as—I had

little to compare it to. Roo coming out of the shower? Once-a-month vanilla bean ice cream?

"Damn," Roo whispered in awe, and I whispered it too. Not a word we were supposed to use. Damn because we hadn't merely imagined the wind. Damn because it seemed like the kind of thing that would get us in trouble. Damn because it was so intensely pleasant, a new item to add to our list of longings.

Something else the wind did, and this I knew because I could look at Roo and see myself: it pinkened our cheeks, it brightened our eyes.

Before we went out we would each be led into a freezer large enough to hold one girl. We had to stay there for sixty seconds, chattering in our sequins, so that when we emerged into the crowd our nipples had the proper quality and we looked adequately forlorn. The customers reacted positively to the combination of sequins and despair. If we shed a tear due to the pain of the freezer it was even better; damp eyes had an enticingly luminous quality. So it was more rebellious not to cry than to cry. Roo and I had discovered a way to control ours. We imagined God's fingers gently pinching the ducts so no tears could emerge, and thus we never cried.

The next day Mrs. Penelope the Mother was flipping flawless pancakes when we came downstairs to eat. She wore a baggy saggy flowered dress and had curlers in her thin hair. She embraced both of us in one hug and then stepped back and looked us over. She smiled kind of sadly, as though she did not quite approve, and we felt awfully guilty. That's why it was a toss-up between Mrs. Penelope the Mother and Mrs. Penelope the Lady. The Lady might make you feel stupid or clumsy, but she'd never make you feel like a disappointment.

"Nice day," Mrs. Penelope said, gesturing to the same flat gray light as always that came through the narrow kitchen windows.

We ate the hot pancakes with lots of butter (Mrs. Penelope the Lady would have been horrified) and, for a short time, felt warm and content.

"Boy," Mrs. Penelope said as we dipped our forks in the leftover syrup on our plates, "I've never seen you girls looking quite so bright-eyed and bushy-tailed."

"It's because—" Roo stopped herself.

"Because why?" Mrs. Penelope demanded. "Because why?"

"Because it's a nice day," I said. "As you said."

Mrs. Penelope eyed us suspiciously, suddenly more Lady than Mother. Roo and I squeezed hands under the big wooden table, stood up, and headed toward the hall closet where our sweaters hung.

"Stop," Mrs. Penelope said. "Have you excused yourselves?"

"May we please be excused, Mrs. Penelope?" we said in unison.

"No you may not," she said. She continued to eye us. "You sit down and stay right there." She stormed out of the kitchen and down the hallway to her suite. We'd never been inside but we'd heard rumors of velvet drapes and jewelry boxes and two hundred pairs of shoes.

Nothing like this had ever happened. Not in ten years had we ever been told to stay at the table after breakfast. We took turns cutting thin, unnoticeable slices from the stick of butter and placing them on our tongues to melt.

The doorbell rang just as Mrs. Penelope the Lady emerged from her suite in a black dress. We poked our heads out from the kitchen. There was a fat policeman on the other side of the door. Mrs. Penelope rubbed up against him. The policeman came toward us with handcuffs and Mrs. Penelope was grabbing us and pinching our upper arms and Roo and I were clinging to each other and crying. But when he handcuffed us *to* each other, we calmed down. Other twins had been separated. We'd heard about it and knew about it and never spoke of it or imagined it.

"My dears," Mrs. Penelope murmured, sticking her head in the window of the police car, for a moment more Mother than Lady, "you shouldn't have seen what you saw. You shouldn't have felt what you felt." She squeezed our cheeks. The policeman squeezed Mrs. Penelope's tits. She gave him a pumpkin doughnut and a travel mug of coffee. We buried our faces in each other's synthetic hair. The handcuffs linking us were chilly on our wrists.

As we passed through the repetitive city blocks, the policeman wanted to play a game. He described each of his buddies—he's got a huge mole on his ear, he's got a tiny wang, he's got a glass eye—and we had to tell him how frequently this guy came to the place and what he asked for and how much he tipped. At first we said we couldn't remember, which was true, because any given customer was as memorable as any individual water droplet that poured over you in the shower, but he was getting cranky so then our memories were jogged and we did remember that one, yes, we did remember that one, big tipper, small tipper, aggressive when drunk, jovial when drunk, et cetera, et cetera, and at every revelation the policeman would give an enormous belly laugh and offer us two peanut M&Ms from a large bag he kept up front.

Then, very shyly, he asked if we remembered him.

Oh yes, yes, we did, hadn't that been a time, boy oh boy, the two of us and him.

Then he got sullen and said how could we remember him if he'd never been there, he was an upstanding family man with two daughters of his own in fact, and were we just a pair of lying little sluts or what, and could he please have back the M&Ms he'd loaned us. Then we got nauseous thinking about all the M&Ms we owed him that were deep inside our guts now.

Eventually the endless gray blocks put us to sleep and when we woke it was sundown. The police car was parked in front of a small lopsided wooden cabin, and across from it an even smaller hut. Beyond the cabin, a grove of trees, like an image from the Internet. The policeman was nowhere to be seen. I would have been scared but Roo's hand was in mine. I tugged on her hand and she turned toward me. Her hair extensions were snarled. Her face was wet and luminous.

"This has been the best day of my life," she whispered.

"Yeah, the best day *ever*," I joked along with her.

But she shook her head at my sarcasm. "The best, best day," she murmured.

"*What?*" I said, pulling my hand away.

"This whole day," she said, her eyes radiant with tears, "we drove out of the city and then we came to a different kind of place."

"I thought you were asleep."

"You were asleep."

I yanked on the door handle.

"Locked," Roo said.

"Shit," I said, expecting Roo to say it simultaneously.

The door of the crooked cabin opened and the policeman came out. It looked like a joke, such a fat man emerging from such a tiny doorway. A small, thin man with black hair and features sharp as pencils followed the policeman. The policeman pounded this man's back in a friendly, exaggerated fashion. We were trained in reading lips because we had to be able to understand a customer's requests even when the place was at full volume; we could interpret desires from across a crowded room. So I could see the policeman saying to the man, "You know what to do."

The thin man came up to the window of the police car. He cupped his hands around his face to look directly in at us. His eyes were urgent, like the eyes of a monster.

The ripe strawberries were clustered among the unripe ones, so each plant required some effort, to harvest the reds without disrupting the greens. For the first row it was not so unpleasant. There was the novelty of kneeling on the damp dirt in the rising sun, which cast light more yellow than gray, and the satisfaction of a huge tin pail beginning to fill with fantastic redness. Even our potato-sack garments held a certain charm. I didn't mind moving down the row on my knees beside my sister, smelling the smell of overripe strawberries, a smell not unfamiliar to us, for we'd had strawberry jam in our day.

Not to mention the eating. We didn't know if it was permitted, but we chose not to ask the thin man, who had awoken us by throwing a rooster into the bunkhouse where there were thirty-nine empty beds and one occupied, by me and Roo, since we always shared. Though the cabin had looked small at first, actually it was a long, low building, and we'd selected a bottom bunk at the end farthest from the door. The rooster marched all the way down the room to us and made his noise right in our ears. When we got out of bed the rooster strutted us over to these potato-sack garments hanging from a pair of hooks on the wall. We pulled off the heavy wool skirts and stiff oxford shirts we'd slept in and pulled on these strange tunics, our torsos goose-bumpy in the dawn. We emerged from the cabin feeling somewhat lighter than we'd felt. The thin man was standing outside with two stacks of tin pails. He smiled at us, revealing sharp, bloodstained teeth, and we almost screamed. He said: "Good morning, Rose and Roo." How dare he know our names. He said it was time to harvest the strawberries. We looked at him blankly. "Harvest" was not a command we'd ever been given. He smiled again—those bloody teeth—and said: "You are correct to be surprised that strawberries are still in season. For a long time I have worked to develop a strain of strawberry plant that produces thrice over the course of the year: May, July, and September." This meant nothing to us and we didn't care, but he seemed proud to have taught us something. He grabbed all the tin pails; it was mildly impressive that such a small, thin man could manage such an awkward load. "Follow me," he said.

So here we were, my sister and I, in the strawberry field, in the crispness of morning, twenty pails to fill and explicit orders about red versus green, more fields spreading out black and green toward groves of trees planted not by a mastermind of city parks but instead just growing that way, their orange and pink leaves fluttering in what we now knew to call *wind, wind* coming off the stream between the fields, and in the distance the rooster a black-and-white dot clawing at the mud amid the tilting wooden structures of the farmyard, and the thin man heading toward the stream with a large knife in the shape of a half-moon. In any case, hungry and not in possession of instructions to the contrary, Roo and I ate strawberries, splendid, and it was then we realized that the thin man's teeth had been stained not by blood but rather by strawberries.

It came swift and sudden up the row, moving fast along the cool dirt, a snake three feet long and as large around the middle as Roo's arm, greenish scales glimmering poisonously. A scattering of strawberries, an overturned pail, we ran, not looking back, crushing strawberries, leaping over rows, down toward the stream where the thin man strolled with his murderous knife, we landed in the thin man's arms, pressed ourselves into his chest so hard that if he'd not possessed his uncanny sturdiness surely we'd have knocked him to the ground. But as it was he held us and smiled upon us with red teeth. He murmured things, I forgot to mention the snakes, my apologies, Roo, my apologies, Rose, they're harmless, overgrown garter snakes, a by-product of the experimental strawberry plants, don't worry, they're everywhere, you'll get used to them, all the while holding the half-moon knife in his left hand. I backed out of his embrace a few seconds before Roo; he touched her hair. When I turned and looked back at the strawberry field, I saw that it was alive with snakes. The whole field undulated with green bodies slithering among red strawberries.

We returned to the strawberry field, our stomachs taut with cold water from the stream. We picked strawberries, filled pails. I attributed my stomachache to the snakes that kept sliding by; only much later would I attribute it to the sight of the thin man stroking my sister's hair extensions. Late in the day, when almost all the pails were full, Roo reached out to touch a snake as it passed. She looked at me, grinned and giggled. My nausea swelled and overflowed. I vomited red water onto a strawberry plant.

My sister and the thin man put me to bed in the bunkhouse. They brought porridge. It was creamy and honeyed, but there was an aftertaste of salt that dried out my mouth and my gut.

My sister didn't sleep with me that night or the next because I was ill; and then, on the third night, when I was better, she still didn't sleep with me. She climbed up the ladder to the bunk above me.

"Roo. What are you doing."

"Going to sleep."

"I'm better now."

"Good."

"Come down!" Ever obedient, she came down. "Sleep here!"

"The mattress is so narrow."

"We always sleep in the same bed."

Roo shrugged and gestured at the abandoned bunkroom, the thirty-nine empty beds, as though to say, *We've only slept together all these years because there was no alternative,* before mounting the ladder once more.

Eventually our hair extensions grew out. The curls began to slide off our dull brownish hair, and soon became so loose we could remove them with the merest tug. These sheddings of synthetic hair got mixed up and mired in the muck of the barnyard, glimmering auburn amid chicken shit.

The thin man said to us, "You have nice hair." We gazed with some longing at our lost curls, sinking in the mud. "I mean the hair on your heads," he said. There were no mirrors on the farm, but I could see Roo's soft straight brown hair fluttering above her eyebrows and feathering at the base of her neck, so I knew my hair was doing the same. The thin man did not compliment us except that once. It was strange to go so long without compliments from men. It was kind of nice and then sometimes not.

In the hut where he slept and where we all ate, the thin man brought out cards after the dinner porridge—playing cards, like those we'd seen a million times at the place, but now we got to handle them and examine them up close. The colorful, regal characters. There were games he taught us, and dried beans for betting. Yet, oddly, I tired long before Roo did—we always used to yawn at the same time, Roo and I—and though I tried hard to fight it so Roo wouldn't be left alone with the thin man, still I'd retire to the bunkhouse early. At night the wind blew tremendously. It kept me up. Then I'd climb the ladder to Roo's bunk but sometimes she wasn't there. I'd pretend she was, putting the pillow just so to imitate the shape of her and clinging to it. I'd get so crazy and scared, like I was a tiny crumb of nothing cowering in the roaring universe. In the morning I'd wake to find Roo in my bunk and me in hers.

"Did you hear that wind?" I said.

"I love it so much," my sister said.

At times I had feelings toward Roo that were unfamiliar to me, and for which I knew no good words, but they were not pleasant.

The thin man played banjo, peculiar songs from faraway, and one night when he pulled the banjo out after dinner, Roo sang along and knew every word of every song.

The thin man taught Roo how to make the daily porridge, which was served at noontime with honey and at nighttime with cheese. Also we ate things grown on the farm. Strawberries, of course, and vegetables from the garden. Soon Roo's porridge surpassed the porridge of the thin man.

One day I looked over at my sister and looked down at myself and realized our appearances had begun to diverge. Roo was plumper now, her breasts larger than mine, her skin a deeper shade of tan. Her hair was light brown and now that my hair was long enough to pull over my shoulder I could see it was several shades darker.

"What color are my eyes?" I said to Roo. Hers were brown flecked with yellow. It was wonderful to have them gazing so thoughtfully into mine.

"Gray," she replied after a moment.

Dismayed, I insisted that we ask the thin man. We stood before him in the barnyard, our eyes wide open.

"Both of you have hazel eyes," he said, and I was filled with giddy relief, "but yours are more gray," he said to me, "while hers are brown like honey."

There were other things, too. Her fingernails grew faster than mine. Freckles appeared on her forehead but not on mine. We noticed a difference in our heights—I perhaps an inch taller—that had been lost on us before. We'd always been so interchangeable that Mrs. Penelope had often just referred to us as R.

Yet still our voices were identical, with the exact same cadence. Still our collarbones were a perfect match.

I couldn't grow accustomed to the wind and I couldn't grow accustomed to the thin man. But I grew accustomed to the snakes among the strawberry plants; I scarcely noticed them anymore and when I did it was with a feeling of fondness.

It was easy to forget certain things about our former life. What was the name of the last street we used to cross before entering the park? What was the weekly breakfast served by

Mrs. Penelope on Wednesdays? Exactly how long did we have to stay in the freezer before going out to the customers?

Time passed. We ate porridge with herbs. I watched a brown bird reclaim a strand of synthetic hair from the freezing mud. Roo and I dug for carrots and placed hay over the dying strawberry plants, working side by side. A series of eerie notes plucked on a banjo, my sister whispering and singing. In the firelight, the Jack of Hearts winking at me. Voices heard as though from afar, the voice of the thin man and the voice of my sister, the same as my voice, but the words drifted over and around me, the fire warming the unpleasant feelings out of me.

One morning they were gone. I woke to the wind, and the rooster scratching. The rooster wandered lonesome over the frozen dung of the barnyard. My sister and the thin man were not in any bed. That was my first thought; I anticipated finding them entangled, I began to understand the vague hatreds I'd felt. It was something of a relief not to discover them, his bed empty and tidy—but they were nowhere else either, not in the fields, not down by the river, not in the groves.

That night it seemed near miraculous to find a letter from my sister tucked under my pillow, how could I have missed it, a note from she whom I had taught to write. Her handwriting still looked like that of a young child, all capitals; her spelling, abysmal.

> R—WE LUV U. HAVE FUN WHAL WE R GONE. KEEP A EYE ON THINGZ. HARVIST

SQUSH/FED CHICKS. THANK U THANK U THANK U. WE LUV U—R

I had never in my life been so enraged; I had never in my life been away from Roo. The loneliest minutes in my life must have been the six before she was born; but those were now trumped by these, as I stormed around the barnyard, crushing the intricate architectures of frosted sludge. Looking out over the strawberry fields, I saw the small plants all turned brown for winter, the snakes vanished, every last bit of redness harvested. Unlike the rooster, I could do something about my resentment. That poor rooster, he was left there in the barnyard digging through the cold mud for auburn curls that might or might not emerge.

Back in the city, no wind blew in the park.

I stood in the middle, right where Roo and I had stood, and looked at the blades of grass and groves of trees. I awaited movement. But the park was still. The sky was gray and quiet, everything bathed in flat city light. The wool skirt weighed on my hips. The starched shirt gripped my throat like a pair of hands.

Mrs. Penelope had greeted me mistrustfully. She was not used to hitchhikers showing up on her doorstep at five in the morning. She wrapped her silken peacock robe tighter around her thin, ladylike frame. "Where's the other one?" she said. Warily, she led me to our old room. Another pair of girls was sleeping in our bed. Mrs. Penelope ordered the elderly maintenance man to bring up a cot. There was no one with whom to share the minor adventures I'd experienced on my journey back to the city, so I let those hours spent traveling slide into gray oblivion.

Our trick for not crying when we had to go into the freezer no longer worked. I couldn't envision God pinching my tear ducts, and I came out crying. But not the desired kind of tearing up that makes one's eyes incandescent; this was true crying, the kind that makes makeup and men run. I kept getting sent back to Mrs. Penelope's with the early shift of girls, those who were less slender or more awkward or partnerless. Pairs of girls were always better off. And pairs of identical twins—well, obviously. The two girls with whom I now shared our old room were new to it, young and scared, which made them irresistible, and they'd creep in quiet, exhausted, hours after I'd settled into my flimsy cot. They were neither friendly nor unfriendly to me, as impeccably gray as the city itself, and mournfully I observed between them the desperate, joyous intimacy I'd once known.

Mrs. Penelope the Lady leaned against the doorframe of the kitchen, luxuriously smoking a cigarette, while I ate undercooked scrambled eggs.

"Do I need to say it?" she said, blowing out.

I looked up at her, terrified.

"You ain't no good no more." It was always a bad sign when Mrs. Penelope slipped into trashy grammar. "Watcha thinkin, hidin in corners all night away from the guys, lettin your makeup run and wearin dirty underwear?"

"When Roo comes back I'll be good again."

"'When Roo comes back I'll be good again,'" she parroted. "She ain't comin back."

"What do you mean?" Hope flooded me. "You know where she is?"

Mrs. Penelope smoked.

"She did all the work fer the both of you."

My fork clattered to the floor. I stood up noisily, pushing my chair back across the linoleum.

"We worked together as identical twins," I hissed, "which is how we brought in all that dirty slutty cash for you, Missy." I couldn't believe I'd called her Missy; that's what she used to call us.

Mrs. Penelope smoked and laughed and for half a second looked a little bit sad.

"Sweetheart, you two ain't identical twins. You ain't even twins. You ain't even *sisters*. Didn'tcha ever notice how you don't look at all alike except fer your size and your hair extensions? In dim rooms men believe anything."

In the park there was a stone bridge built before the climate was controlled. Orange lichen grew on it and beneath it there were places where one could sleep. I thought I was alone but when I woke there were people squeezed in beside me. They had bad breath, it smelled like Coca-Cola and dead squirrels, but they were friendly and didn't mind being held too tightly at night. Soon enough I could out-collect them when it came to five-cent bottles. I found a lighter in a sidewalk grate; we used it to roast the softening eggplants someone discovered behind the grocery. I avoided the other associations I had with eggplant, the darkness of its skin against the tan skin of its harvester. I shat in the pleasant autumnal groves of the park. There was never any wind. My hair became matted, my woolen skirt lighter as its fibers wore away. I tried to pump my heart full of joy. I thought sex under these circumstances was supposed to be wonderful. I tried to develop a particular affinity for one of them, the kind of thing where we might say, The two of us, we're a team, this is our life and we're making it together. We did special things, shared tips about where to find glass bottles and split a candy bar found on the sidewalk and went on nighttime walks not to scavenge but just for fun. We whooped and joked and taunted and smoked discarded cigarettes. But that person disappointed me again and again. In all honesty, this new team didn't hold a candle to the one I'd been on my whole life. I did push-ups and my muscles grew. You're depressed, the vagrants told me. Seriously depressed.

When I rang Mrs. Penelope's doorbell, she refused to let me enter and instead called the fat policeman, as I'd known she would. I didn't protest when he arrived and handcuffed me to myself. Once again we traveled the endless windless city blocks. This time I refused to talk. I refused his peanut M&Ms. "Are you a fucking deaf-mute?" he said.

At sundown, a pregnant woman stood in the barnyard. She wore a white apron and from it she grabbed seed to toss to the chickens clustering around her. In the hut behind her a candle gleamed in a foggy window. This woman was composed of many kinds of roundness: her cheeks, her shoulders, her tits, her belly, her bum. She looked soft to the touch, lovely. The mother everyone yearns for. In the window where the candle glowed a thin man was stirring something in an enormous black pot. I stumbled out of the police car, still handcuffed to myself.

"Why didn't you tell me!" I shrieked.

She looked up and smiled, her eyes drugged with tranquillity. She tried to hurry to me but her body was slow.

"Dearest," she said. Her voice was low and warm, in an unfamiliar register. She had never before called me "Dearest."

"Why didn't you tell me," I squeaked again.

She gestured with her head to the policeman, who strolled over and unlocked the handcuffs and got back in the police car and went back to the city. Then she held me.

"Where did you go?" I moaned into her soft shoulder. "Why did you leave me?"

"Dearest," she said in that odd adult voice. "All those nights we stayed up, playing cards and banjo and everything. You know how Alex and I talked."

"Alex? Who's Alex?" I said.

"How we made plans. The three of us right there at the table."

I remembered myself drifting, not listening, carried upward and away by the warmth of food and fire.

"We knew the baby was coming. We were so eager to get married. We were so grateful to you. How calmly you took it. How generous you were with us, with me. With your love. We were horrified when we got back and you weren't here. We asked the policeman to track you down. And here you are, back at home, dearest, Aunt Rose—"

I stiffened, pulled myself away from her soft, soft body.

"We aren't twins," I said. "We aren't even fucking sisters. We're not related."

In the abandoned bunkhouse the callous wind blew between the cracks. I shared the building with thirty-nine invisible farmhands. In the morning my brain was cold and clear, calm with hatred.

Every time she said "Alex" I couldn't help thinking, "Who's Alex?" She brought me porridge in a wooden bowl, carrying it with both hands like something precious, the bowl an extension of her roundness. Sitting beside the fire, she massaged my hands, as though I was the one about to undergo intolerable physical pain. The warmth of her fingers on mine soothed me into a rare benevolent mood, and I told her she had healing hands; she exchanged a private look with the thin man and I curled my fingers and pulled them away. She asked if I wished to name the baby and I told her I did not. When she questioned me about my time in the city, I overemphasized the loveliness and wildness of the people I'd known in the park, and my tenderness toward them; I enjoyed searching her face for hints of envy. When the baby was ugly and newborn, I heard her fighting with the thin man in the hut. After suppressing my instinct to barge through the door, I couldn't suppress a grin. Once, when she was so exhausted from the baby she went to bed before sundown, I came into the hut and sat beside the fire with the thin man. I wasn't wearing a bra. He played the banjo softly. Slowly I unbuttoned my shirt. My breasts, small and flawless, no crust of dried milk, no distended nipples. He looked up from the banjo and saw what I was showing him. He shut his eyes, but not before I could see disgust and fascination mingling in them; not before the bedroom door cracked open a sliver and then slammed shut. He and I twisted our necks, looking over at the door. I buttoned my shirt and left the hut and went to the windy bunkhouse.

Late at night, more screaming from the hut. A baby screaming, joined by a woman screaming and a man too. In the morning, they were all three exhausted and united. Soon the first snowflake would fall. They came out into the barnyard, the small family, and stood there together huddling under the great heavy sky. A gray wool blanket wrapped around them. They looked at me. Not with hatred but with something else. How humble they were, she and her husband and her child, peasants on the first day of snow. Now she and I looked nothing alike.

Everything I owned could be folded into a single bandanna and so it was. I strode through the barnyard, past the peasants cowering beneath the wool blanket, though I had no idea where I was headed. I set out across the strawberry field, so glaringly empty of snakes, if only she and I were still there, picking strawberries and stroking snakes. I walked for over an hour, my tear ducts out of control and my fingers freezing. Then, miraculously, moments after the snow thickened, I came upon a hut in a grove. It was unlocked, vacant, provisioned with canned foods, dried meat, raisins, oatmeal. There was an indoor pump for water and an outhouse back behind. There was a shovel and an ax and a gun. My loneliness made me brave and mean. This was my place now. I had no qualms about killing its rightful owner. There was a full bookshelf and a bed with a gray blanket. Blue flannel pajamas and a large bag of coffee beans. To my surprise—to my disappointment—no one came to kick me out. All winter I read. I read and I practiced saying "I" rather than "we." Sometimes, in a moment of strength, fortified by beef jerky and canned peaches, I wondered if I might come to love her again. Other times I would lie there whimpering. All the while, the wind blew. I did not look forward to spring.

In spring, when the thaw came, I stepped outside and noticed above the door of the hut a wooden sign: R'S HIDEAWAY. It was obvious that the blanket I'd slept under all winter matched their gray peasant blanket exactly. Enraged, exhausted, I leaned against the dripping hut: I'd never been alone, never been free.

In the strawberry field the plants were coming up bright green. Slim snakes practiced gliding on the cool dirt. I set out across it, preparing for a confrontation.

Please tell me where else I might have gone, what else I might have done.

She stood in the doorway, her face less full of love than it used to be. But still full of love. What she said was, "We need to plant the peas today," and what I said was, "Okay."

Sometimes her daughter can't tell us apart. She comes rushing up the row behind me yelling, "Momma! Momma!" Sometimes she keeps calling me "Momma" even after I twist fiercely around and she sees my eyes, my ferocious mouth, my hair blowing across my face.

CHILDREN

How can I talk about them. The form they chose to take. The pinafore, the suspenders. The broad white collars and the big black buttons.

"*You're* the one who dresses them that way," Thomas would say irritably. "Those are the clothes *you* made. And you are their human *mother.* So enough, okay."

Thomas doesn't believe, and I don't blame him. It isn't easy to believe that when I was sewing those clothes there was something else guiding my fingers, something outside of me, something green and glowing.

I have two of them, a boy and a girl, and they're always looking upward, or almost always, always pointing up, up, branches, birds, planes, moon, stars, *planets,* and there's no way I can keep them inside now that the tornado is here. Their sticky feet rush them down the stairs, out the front door, across the porch, down the steps, across the yard.

I stand in the doorway screeching their names, the human names we gave them when they arrived half a decade ago—*Bill! Lill!*—but they're already past the gate, bound for the road. They look back at me kindly (pityingly?) but continue onward, fast, their bare feet unstopped by the gravel, the lost nails. See, it's just small hints, the toughness of their soft feet, miniature clues—but that's how we know. Or rather, how *I* know, since Thomas doesn't believe, nuzzling their damp heads on watermelon nights in August as though they're children like any others. In the summertime they sweat and glow all night long, those two, and that's another clue right there.

I step out, away from the doorway and onto the porch. The row of trees Thomas planted soon after they arrived is flattening in the wind, I mean *flattening*, and then a handful of tin cans shoots past the house like birds of the future, and my dress is alive with a will of its own, and I cling to the railing and scream for them, but they've already scooted under the barbed wire.

Thomas is yelling something, hanging on to the stone foundation, coming around from the backyard, where he was checking on things. I can't hear him but I know he wants to know where the kids are.

I don't answer him, I keep shrieking their names. They're still within sight, but barely, dark figures on the far side of Field I. The air is green and the wind is clever.

Thomas curses when he spots them. "You couldn't keep them inside."

He's just stating it, he's not accusing me. He knows better than anyone how they are, always talking to each other in a language we don't understand, always putting jam on their hot dogs. They've never belonged to us, not even for a second.

Thomas lets go of the stonework and takes a wind-bashed step across the front yard toward the garage.

"The county said no motor vehicles on the roads," I say, coming down the steps and across the yard behind him. My dress blows up into my face, smothering me.

Thomas yanks me into the cab of the truck. The wind slams the door. I pull my dress away from my face and look at him. He's got a big head, my husband, big like the head of a Saint Bernard, and my head is nothing to sneeze at either. While Bill and Lill have small shapely heads.

"Center Road to Field 5?"

I nod. It's as good a plan as any. They've got to be halfway through Field 3 by now. Thomas puts the truck into reverse.

"This is dangerous," I say.

"Oh yeah," Thomas says. I can't tell if he's agreeing or being sarcastic or what. Isn't it weird how you can be married to someone for eleven years and still not know.

"But maybe not for aliens," I add.

"Spare me," he says.

We've been through this a million times. He refuses to admit what they are. Though they never bleed, not even when they get their vaccination shots or skin their knees. A puncture dot, a raw spot, but never a drop of blood. "Why do they never bleed?" I'll ask him, and he'll say, "They never bleed because they're our kids and they're tough as nails."

But the reason they never bleed is because of their skin. Sure, it's a subtle enough thing, it's not like you'd pick them out of a crowd of kids, but when you're the one who bathes them and lotions them and scratches their backs as they fall asleep, you know these things, and I know that their skin has a plastic quality, a durability far greater than mine.

I've overheard Thomas telling the guys that I'm crazy, on that front at least. I love her to death, but. She thinks the kids are aliens.

Aw, hell, Mark or Matthew or Tim or whoever says, putting his feet up on the porch railing. Yeah. My kids are aliens too. God, they're monsters. They're zombies. Hell, I don't know what they are. Trolls.

And I go silently about my planting or weeding or whatever while my aliens do somersaults on the grass around me like any other kids. His ability to deny them is a testament to their artful, maybe even desperate, efforts to blend in.

"You know," Thomas says now, making the sharp right onto Center Road, "if you keep talking this way about the kids, one of these days I'm going to have to leave you."

Thomas will never leave me, but before I get the chance to say it, a raccoon flies across the road. The creature seems surprisingly calm, soaring alongside a cluster of dirty napkins. I look at Thomas and Thomas looks at me. If this tornado can lift a twenty-pound mammal off the ground, what does that mean for our two forty-pounders?

Their slender skeletons, their halos of wild hair. Their oversized eyes.

Because let me be clear: them being different doesn't mean a thing. It's just a funny little fact about them, a little secret I know, the way you'd know if your kid still wet the bed or sucked her thumb in third grade. Do I worry sometimes that it'll become a problem someday, that their nature will make itself known at the wrong times, that they'll be filled with cosmic longings impossible to satisfy? Well, yes, of course. But for now it's harmless enough.

The wind pushes against the truck like a giant palm. Thomas and I have a duet of muttering and cursing and hoping as he steers past Field 3.

"There!" Thomas shouts.

They're not running anymore, they're standing in the dead center of Field 5 like aliens awaiting their long-lost spaceship.

And I begin to panic for real. I've known all along, with a mother's knowledge, that they'll survive the tornado. They've done more daredevil things than I can count, things involving sleds, tire swings, train tracks, this disregard for their physical safety another hint of what they really are, but I've never considered the possibility that they might leave me. That they might actually pick up and head back to wherever they came from. They're mine, through and through, and I don't care a bit about the rules of some other planet—I've loved them and raised them with the best love there can be on any end of the universe, so help me.

In the height or depth of my labor, when everything was blurry and impossible, when I was vomiting and humming and the sky was day and night and day and night at the same time, I found myself suddenly calm, perched on a narrow precipice of calm, and here they came, luminous twin bubbles floating toward me in a beam of green light that overmastered the hospital's fluorescence, and I opened my mouth and the beam sizzled on my tongue and deposited there its greenish gift and I swallowed the two elegant bubbles, and the calm was gone and I had to hum and hurt and hum and hurt for a while longer, and then they were stuck, halfway in and halfway out, and the nurse said, *Feel the head! Feel the head!*, and I felt a head, and it felt sublime, it felt wrong to feel a head coming out of yourself like that, and then they were born all at once, both of them within ninety seconds, my tiny perfect children, a detonation in my heart. I'll never know what happened to the other pair of twins I carried for nine months, whether the aliens infected them with their alien souls, or whether they replaced them altogether, or whatever.

But anyway, from that very first instant, I was fierce about them. The clichés don't begin to do it justice—I'd throw myself in front of any bus, I'd give them every garment off my back, I'd drain myself dry over and over again, forever, gladly.

Though Bill and Lill have never needed such gestures from me. They've been self-sufficient from the get-go, they've always owned themselves. Sure, they're affectionate enough with us—they'll nuzzle up against us when they get drowsy, and when they were babies they'd crawl over to us croaking *Mamama Dadada* in their brand-new voices. But there's always been a line in the sand, a not-needing, as though we're just icing on the cake. When they were toddlers they'd pick things up off the floor, a piece of thread or a crumb, and slowly, blissfully examine whatever it was for so long that I got scared. No matter how many times I called their names, they remained focused, showering the pebble, the key, the spoon with more attention than they'd ever shown me or Thomas. And when they sleep, their faces become so still and solemn, their limbs so shiny, that I can tell they're traveling far away, to ingest the mercury or radiation or whatever it is they need.

Here, now, in the middle of Field 5, they laugh up at the tornado like bullies, their broad white collars plastered to their skinny necks. Thomas parks the truck askew and we leap out and run across the field with the wind pushing us forward, and I feel hot and cold, hot and cold, and they're waving at us like we've just showed up for a picnic. A tennis racket swirls above them, a frying pan, a flowerpot. We're halfway to them when the wind flips on us and then it becomes as hard as walking in a rowdy crowd. We have to elbow our way toward them, but I don't mind fighting through something to get to them, I always feel that way anyhow.

They're holding hands, hopping up and down, the wind blurring their faces, twisting and torturing every sound they make.

"NA!" Lill screams.

"DO!" Bill screams.

"TOR!"

"NA!"

"DO!"

The exact second I realize, with knee-weakening relief, that it's human syllables they're shouting—it's right then that the sheet of corrugated metal shoots across Field 5, shoots as if someone shot it from a gun, it comes so swift and sudden, bisecting the field, skimming fast toward Bill and Lill, slicing the slim bellies of my aliens. I grab my own midsection, it's as though I myself have been cut, my dress ripped open, my gut ripped open—the twins sink to the ground, blood seeping out all around them, I'm beside them as if by magic, as if I teleported the twenty feet dividing me from them, I'm trying to gauge how badly they're damaged, I'm holding the pieces of them together, the flaps of skin beneath her sliced pinafore, his sliced suspenders, Bill's wound in my left hand, Lill's in my right. It's not for nothing I took those nursing classes—quickly I determine that their cuts are not as deep as they seem, which is a very good thing, because I have no way to acquire transfusions of alien blood, this gooey blood with its uncanny glow, my hands all syrupy now with its brightness.

They aren't crying—another hint, as if any more are needed—but instead gaze up at me with strained, shocked, enormous eyes. Their lean arms, their lean legs, small bleeding stars against the wheat and the dirt. We're crouched down so low to the ground that the wind can't find us.

"Are we dead?" Lill wants to know.

"Not at all!" I tell her. "Not even a little bit."

"Mamamama," Bill says.

"Billyboy," I say. "Lillylady."

Only then do I remember Thomas. I look over my shoulder, assuming he's inches behind me, his hands itching to comfort and to hold. But he's still twenty feet back, down on his knees, his arms crisscrossed over his chest.

It's the blood, the first-ever sight of the blood, that's done it. Never mind that I've been telling him. Never mind that they need him now, that we need to carry them back to the truck and make our way through the tornado and get home, where I can sew them up just fine and give them hot dogs with jam and put them to bed so they can visit their galaxy and fetch whatever it is they need to survive.

"Thomas!" I shout. I know he's the easygoing kind of guy who can adjust to anything. Why else would I have married him? Life is long. "Come here, T."

But he's stuck. He's staring at them like they are wrong.

Noticing (noticing, they're always noticing) their daddy's dread, Lill and Bill meet his stare.

"Daddy?" they request.

But he stays put.

"*Daddy,*" I command.

"They're glowing." He's shaking his head.

"Who's glowing?" Lill says.

"And their *blood* is *green.*" He blinks too many times.

"Whose blood is mean?" Bill says.

"Yeah, they're *aliens,*" I try to mouth to him so they won't understand. But nothing gets past those two.

"Aliens," they murmur, looking down at themselves in wonder, examining their smudged limbs.

"You won't melt," I yell at Thomas, whose arms remain crossed over his chest. "You won't die or be poisoned or turn into an alien or anything."

He keeps staring.

"Believe me," I say, "I've tried everything. I've tasted their saliva and licked their eyelids. I've swallowed bits of their hair and I've spread their snot on my forearms."

Bill and Lill laugh that same mysterious laugh they'd laughed at my belly button when they were little. They'd crawl over to me and pull up my shirt and put their lips against my belly button as though they were doing mouth-to-mouth. Another hint, of course—that fascination with and amusement at their humble human mother.

Still on his knees, Thomas leans away from their laughter.

"Their skulls," he chokes.

"Whose skulls?" Lill stops laughing to ask him this, almost coldly.

"Who's dulls?" Bill echoes.

I know what Thomas means. Times like this, when they get laughing, you can see the blood vessels on their foreheads swelling, pulsing eerily.

But those pulsing heads are resting exquisitely against my hip bones and my fingers are pinching together the flaps of their sliced tummies as tight as tight can be.

"It doesn't matter," I say to him.

I look down at my two, my Bill and my Lill, and see that they have already forgiven him, that they've already forgiven me, that their forgiveness stretches backward and forward toward a distant universe.

Thomas, though, keeps his arms crossed over himself until the moment when he lets the wind knock him onto all fours, and he crouches there in Field 5 like a beast, an earthly creature through and through.

And then, slowly, crawling beneath the force of the wind, he comes toward us, hand knee hand knee hand knee hand knee hand, until his fingertips touch the oozing, shimmering blood that's already begun to turn the soil into a new kind of mud.

THE WORST

Other, terrible things had happened, but this was the worst: a Friday night and we had free tickets to either a 6:30 or 8:30 movie, so, after meeting on a frigid street corner beside a cold golden statue of either a pregnant woman or a bull, we went to the theater and discovered that one movie was about child prostitutes in Bangladesh and the other was silent. Don't get us wrong, we like silent movies, but already the world was silent enough. It had been silent for days now. Even though the pretty girl at the counter assured us: *There will be music, there will be live music, a live musician,* still the word "silent" stuck with us and we couldn't bear it so we left. Abandoned by our plans, our images of "a movie in Manhattan," maybe "dinner at a diner afterward," we had nothing to cling to but our swiftly fading conviction that we could make fun anywhere, out of anything, like people who make love in the laundry room or station wagon. We walked up the cold boulevard commenting on dresses in store windows (but it was too cold to look at such dresses, I had to turn away from the sight); we welcomed an alternate sight, the sight of a cathedral, until we noticed the men dying on the steps of it. They weren't dying, not really, I guess, but then again we're all dying. The dying men burrowed into dirty sleeping bags. Then: a hotel. Walk in like you own the place, like you don't have holes in the crotch of your jeans where your thighs rub against each other, like your shoelaces aren't dirty with dog shit, et cetera, like you're wearing lipstick rather than Vaseline. You'll see the lobby is made of pure gold. That vase containing a hundred burgundy roses—it takes up far more space in the world than you, it produces far more beauty than you, you shrink before it. Crumpled up this way, I ruined the illusion that we owned the place, now we'll never know how much more gold, how many more roses, we might have seen in the bathrooms off the lobby; we left with aching bladders. There was one last thing we could do: a store where I had sometimes been known to purchase something like a normal person. Limping with failure, we approached that store. What it had was clothing of many colors and what I wanted was clothing of many colors. I fingered the sweaters. Help me, I beg of you, help me. It was then that it happened, right then, the worst part, my hand touching many different sweaters at once: royal blue, heather gray, bubblegum pink, traffic cone orange, despair. They play loud, confusing music in this store, music designed to alter the electricity that dictates your desires. It goes without saying: we left empty-handed. Don't dare look back at the racks as you exit.

HOW I BEGAN TO BLEED AGAIN AFTER SIX ALARMING MONTHS WITHOUT

I saw her on the bus and she disgusted me even then. She was eating something out of a clear plastic container. Something white and liquidy, yet she was eating it with a fork. I could not tell what manner of thing it was. Animal? Vegetable? Mineral? There were small chunks in the white liquid. I imagined playing Twenty Questions with her. Does it involve tuna? Does it involve mayonnaise? Is it sweet? Is it salty? Is it meant to be served hot? Is it meant to be served cold? Is it kosher? She tipped the container toward herself as she ate and the white liquid started to drain out one corner onto her black nylon tracksuit. Eventually she noticed what she'd done and it brought a smile to her face. Not a smile of shame, I might add. When I once again looked over, she had something unidentifiable in her mouth, clenched between her teeth, about to be torn open. My intestines seized in horror—with what strange food would she confront us now? Slowly, though, I came to see the thing in her mouth for what it was: a small square packet containing a single wet wipe.

But it was not only the white food; also I could tell she was having her period. Her face had that combined flush and pallor, at once swollen and sallow. Such an internal, indecipherable thing, you might think, yet I can always identify a menstruating woman, particularly in the unkind glare of public transportation after dark.

All that, just on the bus, and meanwhile I had problems of my own.

And then, when it came time to switch to the train, she too got off the bus. She too climbed up all the many stairs to the elevated station. The outward-bound platform was abandoned but for me and her, the white substance now turning cold and flaky on her black tracksuit, surely giving off the odor of wet wipe combined with tuna fish—though I'd never dare get close enough to smell it myself. Across the tracks, on the inward-bound platform, a pair of teenagers kissed and clung to each other and kept warm. It was the first cold night. I tried not to be inordinately envious, except of the faux-fur-lined hoods on their jackets.

I walked down the platform, away from the kids and away from her. Beneath the elevated station, the most enormous graveyard in the city. It stretched for blocks in every direction, releasing only negligible smells and sounds. A hint of grass in the process of freezing. The hum of a passing truck, miniature echoes among the tallest headstones. It was a grand place, the graveyard, and I liked to look out over it. I liked to search for headstones with my name on them; if the lettering was large, it was easy enough to read from the platform, and I'd found my surname more than once. But that was a game for daylight. Alongside the outer edge of the graveyard, a sports field with six towering fluorescent floodlights. The field seemed to float above the graves. The grass was still bright green. The shirts of the players glowed red and gold. It was hard not to mistake their far-off, anxious, screaming voices for the voices of young zombies emerged from the graveyard to play soccer.

But get this: she had followed me all the way down to the dark end of the platform. She stood not more than eight feet from me. I should mention that she was pretty and young. I attempted to feel an affinity for her, an affiliation, but it was not possible. Too fresh in my memory was the image of her slimy fork and menstrual face. It seemed we ought to acknowledge each other, two young women amid all this desolation, but instead I looked away. In the distance, a suspension bridge stretched over gleaming black water. Not that I could see the water, since many ugly things blocked it, yet I could imagine it, dark and oily in the night, multicolored with the frenetic task of reflecting the city. Atop the enormous steel structure from which the suspension bridge hung: two blinking red lights. Usually it's a lovely thing to see blinking lights from afar, yet these lights I did not enjoy; they did not blink at a pleasant pace. They should have gone blink—blink—blink, but instead they went blinkblinkblink. I turned my attention back to her. She stood there, motionless, perhaps staring at the blinking red lights. I leaned out over the track to check for the headlights of an approaching train. There they were, still several stations away. Perhaps she too leaned out over the track and spotted the remote train; whatever the cause, something changed, something compelled her, because suddenly she was stepping toward me. There was nothing to do but meet her eyes. As I mentioned, she was young and pretty, with a friendly face, and it was not as much of a strain to smile at her as I'd imagined. I awaited her innocuous question: Excuse me, do you have the time? Excuse me, how many stops to Sheepshead Bay? Excuse me, does this line connect to the B? Excuse me, is this the inbound or outbound? Excuse me, but where did you get those jeans?

Watching her step closer, I wondered if we could have been friends.

Or maybe it would be something slightly less innocuous than a question—a statement. God, it's cold. I saw you on the bus. Ah to be a teenager in love. Thank God the train's coming. It's creepy here by the graveyard.

She stopped near enough that I could see the crusty whiteness at the corners of her mouth. I turned my gaze to her feet and anticipated her voice; high and cheery, I guessed.

"I really" (high and cheery indeed) "grossed you out on the bus, didn't I?"

I looked up at her, disbelieving, my heart going swift and hard. How dare she notice, how dare she accuse me.

"It's one of my grandmother's specialties, in case you were wondering."

Her eyes were bloodshot. I watched the poor capillaries

doing the best they could. I prepared myself to inform her that she had not grossed me out at all. But then my heart started to mess around, as it had tended to do in recent months, shivering and jabbing inside me.

"Anyway," she continued, sparing me, "this is kind of awkward, but do you have a tampon I can borrow? I'm desperate."

First: I was right! Second: Where would she go to insert this tampon? Third: A tampon cannot be *borrowed*. Fourth: I had an unopened box in my bag. Fifth: I remembered him in the fluorescent drugstore asking me what was the point of buying tampons, given the situation.

"Sure." I attempted joviality. "As long as you promise not to return it."

She grinned. I laughed nervously.

"I knew you'd be the right person to ask." She said this in a scary, meaningful way, and my fingers were quivering as I unzipped my bag and pulled out the brand-new box of tampons and tried to break through the packaging. Meanwhile the train was approaching, she was staring at me, the plastic continued to defy me, I yanked out a pen, she stared at me like she knew something, I jabbed the pen at the plastic, the plastic gave way, I grabbed and peeled.

It was a merciful moment, the moment when I finally placed a tampon in her palm. The sacred white tube. I added a second, a third.

My period had not been coming. It did not come, and it did not come, and it did not come, it did not come, it did not come. This was not due to pregnancy; if only. There were other, sadder factors at play.

"Thank you," she said, and then, "thank you, thank you," as I added each additional tampon. It crossed my mind that perhaps she was just a normal girl. "I'm so desperate," she said. "You really saved the day." But then I became certain that she wanted to hurt me, because she kept going on about her gratitude, through her gratitude implying the richness of her flow, and surely my envy must have been there on my face, yet still she went on. The train was getting near, and I wanted—needed—it to arrive, to bear me away from this moment.

"The zombies are playing awful hard tonight, aren't they?" she said, pointing toward the playing field where the green grass was beginning to freeze over. They ran back and forth across it, a smear of great brightness in even greater darkness. I listened to their voices, screams of victory and screams of defeat. Even from this distance it was possible to see the blue tinge to their skin. I shivered; she could read my mind.

The train screamed its way into the station, drowning out the sounds of the soccer-playing zombies. The bleeding girl said one last thing to me, though I will never be sure, because the train was screaming right beside us: "You always give something up to get something else."

When the doors of the train opened I rushed into the car ahead of the one she boarded. We could not be together for another second. Yet I knew she was there, standing at the front of her car, looking through the windows, staring at the back of my neck. I forgot to mention that I'd noticed a tattoo on her neck. A gray smear of something anatomical, an anatomical heart or plant or something.

A train passed on the track beside us, another outbound

train, going slightly faster in the same direction. The sign read OUT OF SERVICE and as the train pulled ahead of us I observed that there was nobody on it except in one car a figure in a blue uniform. This person was wearing a blue winter hat and I stared hard, trying to figure out if the hat was part of the uniform or if the employee had done a very thorough job matching the hat to the uniform. Then, as he turned his head, I saw that the figure in the uniform had the face of a wolf. The wolf gave me a glimpse of his face, not meeting my eyes, and then turned back to his original position. Did he give half a nod to someone in the car behind mine?

But when I twisted around to check, I was shocked to discover that she wasn't standing at the window as I had pictured.

There were only four other passengers in my car, afloat in sleep. No one had seen what I'd seen, and I did not scream.

Just then a small bubble of blood emerged from deep inside me. It appeared on the cusp, beneath my underwear beneath my jeans, and quietly popped. The sound of a minuscule kiss. Followed by a brief yet definite rush. By the time I got off the train at my stop I was crying with gratitude. My face wet. I walked into November. A car that in another life would have accelerated through the yellow stoplight and killed me did not accelerate and kill me. Alive and bleeding, I arrived at my doorstep to find that his name had been rubbed off the tag beneath our doorbell.

THE BEEKEEPER

People and things are disappearing in the city. These people are girls between the ages of eleven and seventeen who have not yet been stiffened by life in skyscrapers, who have not yet donned the hood and trousers, who, in a different era, would have been milkmaids, weavers, beekeepers. These things are objects the aforementioned girls have used. A brush, for instance, containing loose strands of hair. Bedsheets slept between, bath towels wrapped around, slippers slid into. Pencils gnawed upon, notebooks written in, magazines flipped through. A spoon used to eat soup, a fork used to shovel food, a knife used to spread or to cut.

This is why, notwithstanding the dangers one may encounter outside the city, Maebh's parents are sending her to The Farm, and have ordered me to go with.

"If you had to choose," Maebh says, "which would you hate least: to have spiders crawling all over you, or rats, or snakes, or frogs, or bees?"

She sticks her skinny leg out the window of the car—yes, the car—which I am steering through the countryside—yes, the countryside—past the orchard—yes, the orchard. It is hot late afternoon and fragrant with rotting fruit. A circumstance unimaginable to anyone from the city. Unimaginable to me three days ago. I feel drunk.

"I do not know," I say. She has been asking me these kinds of questions throughout the entire journey; I do not think she is cruel, and I do not think she intends to highlight the vast differences between us, but still she is constantly doing so. Unlike her, I have not been to The Zoological. I do not know what a spider is, not really, nor a rat, nor a snake, nor a frog, nor a bee. In the city we do not have such exotic creatures. I have only seen moving pictures of these animals.

"Come on," she says, flicking her pearly toenails against the side-view mirror. "You gotta pick one. Spiders, rats, snakes, frogs, or bees?"

"Rats," I say. "Because they are mammals." This, at least, is a fact I have learned.

"Hm," she says. "Good point."

At times, she sounds nearly thoughtful. She brings her leg back into the car, wraps her arms around her knees, and crouches on the seat. I have already told her to buckle up; she has already refused.

"I'd choose bees," she says. "Definitely bees. Easy."

"But they sting," I say. Again, a fact I have learned.

"They make honey," she says. A fact I once knew but forgot; upon being reminded of it, I wish I too had chosen bees over rats, but this is not the sort of thing one confesses to a girl like Maebh.

At The Farm, there are many bees. They are large and fuzzy. They wander dazed among the wild grapevines that have netted Main House, among the waist-high grasses in the yard (well, waist-high for me and thigh-high for Maebh), among the unknown fruits that dangle off the trees with bronze bark. Maebh tells me these are called plums and laughs at me for not recognizing them.

"They're what prunes come from! You didn't know that?"

The sun itself is like honey here, thicker and more orange as the August afternoon matures. I am surprised to find that I can sit on the porch in a rocking chair, relaxing into the heat and the smell of orchards, without fear. I would not have guessed that I would be capable of forgetting about the dangers; I have never before left the city. I have never before encountered "pollen" (the word Maebh uses for the soft dust), nor a stream of water like the one that runs behind Main House. I have seen streams of hot chocolate in the grand supermarkets, and streams of beer in the pubs, but never this, clear and lazy, with small colorful stones on the bottom.

Maebh lies down on the sun-soaked floorboards of the porch. She tells me she is filled with nostalgia. I am not surprised—I am only surprised that she has such a word in her vocabulary—because as we were leaving the city this morning her parents told me they used to bring her here every summer when she was a very young child, in the years before the dangers.

Suddenly she jumps up and steps through the tall grass toward the stream. I watch from the porch. She kneels and slaps water all over her face, shrieking with the cold of it. Then she starts to unbutton her blouse and wiggle out of her jeans. Is she going to—bathe?—swim?—dive? Showering, that's how I've encountered water.

Maebh turns back to look at me. I am trying to not look at her. She re-buttons her blouse and re-zips her jeans.

"Later," she says. "I'm hungry now. I'm thirsty. Wanna drink milk?"

The house has been provisioned by an old farmer and his wife. Maebh's parents deposited an unnecessarily large sum into this farmer's bank account and told him to make sure we have food until the disappearances cease, or until Maebh heads back to boarding school in Japan come September.

There is milk in the refrigerator—yes, a real refrigerator, pale green with rounded edges, which wheezes and thunks all day long—and a huge circular loaf of bread on the table, and four jars of preserves. I read the labels: apple, okay, pear, okay, plum again, the source of prunes, apparently, and gooseberry. Gooseberry! Well, I can at least guess what that is; I am familiar with strawberries and blueberries. Maebh finds two old jam jars in the cupboard and pours milk into them. It is pleasant to watch her pouring it. I ought to be pouring milk for her. She hands me my milk and we carry everything out to the porch.

I have never tasted anything like this milk. It is better than beer, better than margarine, better than orange juice. Maebh says it comes from cows that were probably milked this morning, or maybe last night. This milk has never been powdered; there are no soybeans involved. Between the two of us we drink half a gallon. We rip hunks off the loaf of bread and dip them into the preserves. The plum and gooseberry are too rich for my taste, but I am fond of the pear. Maebh does not like pears, so I get it all. I shove bread deep into the jar to reach the last bit. When I look up, I see that she is watching me.

"I didn't know you were fun," she says.

There are many bedrooms at The Farm. It seems I ought to stay in one of the outlying buildings, where the family's servants have historically slept. But the farmer's wife prepared two bedrooms side by side in Main House. I do not know if Maebh's parents requested this arrangement, or if the farmer's wife decided on her own, but we shall go along with it because everywhere else is covered in pollen. The farmer's wife made the beds with white wool blankets, and put jugs of daisies on the bureaus, and spread rag rugs on the floors. All of this makes Maebh gasp with delight. If I ever expressed myself in gasps, I am sure I would gasp too.

"Night-night," Maebh says, lolling against the doorjamb for an instant before slipping into her dark bedroom.

"Good night," I say, before retiring into mine.

We had no proper dinner, but are still overfull with bread and milk. It is uncannily easy to fall asleep.

It is barely light when Maebh wakes me, stomping her foot outside my door. I understand more than ever why Maebh's parents believe she is a prime target for these odd disappearances, even though she is nearly eighteen and thus almost out of danger, on the verge of donning her hood and trousers. It is always the wildest girls, the most vigorous and lean, those who enjoy stretching on the roofs of the skyscrapers, those who behave as though they are immune to the dangers.

I get out of bed and start to put on my hood and trousers, my fingers stumbling over the buttons and snaps. Maebh stomps her foot a second time, a third. When I finally emerge, Maebh grabs my hand. We have never before touched. I am aware of this. Maebh is not. Her blinding yellow sundress. She leads me down the stairs and out into the grass, which is wet.

"Did it rain last night?" I say, unable to control the thrill in my voice. It has been so long since there was rain in the city. I was only a child then.

"No," she says. "That's dew. It happens every night in the countryside. You hardly know anything, do you?"

She really is a little bitch but it is not her fault.

When we get to the stream she slips out of her sundress. I avoid looking at her body. This is just my job. I will stand here to make sure she does not drown. Not that I could help her if she did, since I have never swum, nor taken a bath. In any case.

"You too!" she commands, up to her ankles in water so cold she cannot breathe.

It takes me much longer to undress than it took Maebh. There are so many buttons and snaps on my trousers, and my hood is tightly laced. She has gotten in all the way by the time I join her. The frigid water on my shins makes me feel as though I have drunk ten cups of coffee. Yet somehow I am not frightened. Maebh's curly blond hair has become brown and straight now that it is wet. This makes her appear more solemn, which I appreciate.

"Get in all the way," Maebh instructs.

"No," I say, "thank you."

"I command you to get in all the way," she says.

I try to maintain my impassive face, straight mouth and neutral eyes, but it is not easy. An unpleasant sensation swells inside me at the sight of her mouth, left open after she spoke the word "way," her lower lip hanging down, her jaw loose in the casual manner of those accustomed to power.

"Just kidding!" she yelps, plunging her head underwater. She clings to handfuls of pebbles in the streambed and lets the water wash over her. She wriggles in the current. She splashes and surfaces. I am careful to keep my eyes off her body. It is not hard to imagine, after all: narrow hips and thighs, hard dark nipples and a rib cage like old architecture.

"I can look at you but you can't look at me!" Maebh says.

I cannot tell if I am more startled by her jubilant rudeness or by the conviction that she has perceived my thoughts. I feel her staring, and long for my hood and trousers.

"God," she says, "you're so *smooth* everywhere."

Maebh's parents thought it wisest to send a person of unspecified gender along to keep an eye on their daughter. It is widely believed that we are asexual.

Our days are characterized by bees, by sunlight, by pollen, by water, by overripe fruit, by Maebh teaching me things she assumes someone eight years older ought to know. *That's just a spiderweb! Mud won't make your toenails rot. Outside the city the temperature can vary more than twenty degrees. Hear the frogs?*

The farmer and his wife are frightened of people from the city, and leave provisions in the earliest hours of the morning while we are still asleep. We wake to find milk and yogurt and cheese and nuts and bread and preserves and honey on the heavy wooden table in the kitchen.

Sometimes Maebh goes hours without looking directly at me; other times she stares at me so intently that I feel as though her eyes are penetrating through to the inside.

The Farm is two hundred acres. A barbed wire fence encircles all its overgrown orchards and neglected fields. I hold in my palm animals I have only ever seen on a computer screen. Ladybugs are the most charming example, but also snails, daddy longlegs, dung beetles.

I do not live in the state of terror I anticipated when Maebh's parents proposed that, for a sum equivalent to five years' wages in my position as head window-washer of their skyscraper, I accompany their daughter out of the city, beyond the dome, to the ancestral farm where, in a different era, their grandparents lived the good honest life of the earth.

It is possible—in fact, it is impossible not—to forget about the dangerous times in which we live.

Meanwhile, the disappearances continue in the city, and are occurring ever more frequently. Maebh's parents command us to stay in the countryside and to enjoy The Farm.

They thank me profusely, and apologize for the fact that this is lasting longer than expected.

Eventually, I—even I, who have always been careful of the days, who have kept a weekly calendar, who have measured out the hours with three clocks in a one-room apartment on the lowest level of an unclean skyscraper—lose track of time. I ask myself, is today the 11th? 15th? the 17th? the 22nd? the 29th?, grateful that I do not know.

We suck on blades of grass. We let our feet harden and get muddy. We find strawberries growing in glens. We notice ornate tapestries of moss and lichen on the rocks at the westernmost edge of the property. We see the clouds puffing themselves up into creatures that fill half the sky. We lie on the porch watching the bees weave through the late afternoon. Only rarely do they sting us, and when they do we do not mind. Some days I am more of a boy and some days I am more of a girl. We hardly talk, and then sometimes we do.

"I should've been born in a different time," Maebh says, grinding a blade of grass between her molars, reclining on the hot wooden floorboards of the porch, her breasts flattening beneath her sundress as she stretches her arms above her head.

This is how Maebh is, I know that now. She frequently says this kind of thing. The kind of thing that is full of longing. She is thoughtful, nostalgic, and melancholy, all the traits I have valued most in my twenty-five years. She is not flippant (though every morning at the stream she sprays me with frigid droplets from her hair and grins when I wince) nor foolish (though whenever she starts dancing to the music inside her head I wonder if she has filled too much of her brain with those shows teenage girls watch) nor spoiled (though she does get angry whenever she is hungry), nor immature, nor unkind, nor any of the things I anticipated.

"We both should have," I say eventually.

"Both should have what?" she says. Maebh is not accustomed to me saying anything that goes beyond the obligations of my job.

"We both should have been born in a different time," I say.

"Oh, yeah." She shuts her eyes and smiles. "Tha's right," she coos. "We both shoulda been born in a different time. I coulda been a milkmaid. You coulda been a beekeeper."

"I could have been a farmer," I say, wishing to keep up. "You could have been a weaver."

"Oh yeah," Maebh says.

The next morning, we wake to find on the kitchen table a message from Maebh's parents, which requests that we return to the city six days from now so Maebh can pack for boarding school, as August has almost come to an end.

On our fourth-to-last day, the bees disappear. There are only a few left, buzzing weakly above the long grasses, barely clearing the surface of the stream. Maebh is upset.

"Well damn," she says, stomping through fields that have not been cultivated in half a century.

She is convinced that the bees have some secret hideout on some far corner of the property to which they are retiring now for fall. All day I follow Maebh around as she searches for the winter palace of the bees. She says she will be fine if she just knows where they are. We do not return to Main House till after dark. By then, there are only two bees lolling around the porch. We are dehydrated, our skin cut by brambles and rashes emerging on our legs. Maebh plunks herself down in the rocking chair and I stand, nervous, in the doorway. I have never seen her so mad and so sad.

"Maebh," I say, desperate to distract her. "What an unusual name."

"Irish," she says.

"Yes?" I say politely.

"It means: she who intoxicates."

I grip the doorjamb.

She who intoxicates.

"My parents," she says. She sighs. "They have dumb ideas. *B-h?* How's anyone supposed to know how to pronounce that?"

She looks out at the night, which already smells like dew. She has passed into that indifferent mode of hers.

"I'm going to sleep," she says.

"I am going to sleep," I echo.

Maebh comes into my bedroom very early the next morning. Immediately I am fully awake, my skin burning. I believe that this is it, that she will lie down beside me on the white sheet and everything will begin. But she hovers in the doorway.

"Quick!" she says.

Her voice, her urgency, her sundress. I reach for my trousers.

"No! Don't!" she says. "Not necessary."

Though I have often neglected to wear my hood at The Farm, I have never gone without trousers. The day is warm already—Indian summer, another phrase Maebh taught me—and it is not uncomfortable to be naked. Perhaps this is how she wants it to begin, in the tall dewy grass.

"Quick!"

I follow her down the path to the old orchard, which was overgrown at first but has been cleared by our feet. I am not one to tremble but I am trembling. She leads me to a twisted plum tree and points at a single woozy bee wavering around a speckled plum.

"Watch," she whispers.

I stare at the bee. But it makes me dizzy. I look up at the strange silver clouds of morning, wondering how exactly it will begin.

"Watch!" she orders.

I obey, and suddenly there's something halfway between a flash and a snap, an instantaneous flicker, and nothingness where the bee had been.

This is just how every disappearance is described in the newspapers. The swiftness of it, the sound and the light, and—

I never thought to worry about the possibility that the disappearances might come to the countryside. I always assumed Maebh's parents knew something I didn't about the scope of the calamity.

Maebh stares, her face radiant and dark (how much sun we have taken here!), at the place where the bee just vanished.

We do not send any message to Maebh's parents. We do not tell the farmer there will soon be a disaster here. We do not talk about anything beyond The Farm. I wish I could say that we share a bed, or that we tell each other certain things. However, I can say we spend enough time lying on the porch with our bare arms flung above us that I memorize the pattern of the long brown hairs in Maebh's armpits. I do not ask Maebh if she is scared. I know her well by now and I observe that she is not. She is waiting.

We enjoy large quantities of milk and preserves. Maebh consumes them with even greater zeal than before. Sometimes I am on the cusp of reaching out to stroke her. More than once I come close to blurting something. The words are right there, already in my mouth, swirling around on my tongue. But always Maebh stands up just then, or rolls away, or falls asleep.

These plums. This light.

On the day before we are supposed to return to the city, at that time when the sunlight gets richer and darker with each passing second, Maebh is wading through the grass ahead of me—the grass that only comes up to her thigh, that comes all the way up to my waist—carrying a rock we found, a rock covered in green moss and orange lichen as though someone decorated it. I am keeping an eye on Maebh. I do not think of her thighs as thighs—in my mind, I call them haunches. *Haunches,* that is the word in my mind when it happens.

The snap and the flash. The flash and the snap. The colorful rock thudding to the ground. The air into which she disappears—it does not even shimmer. There is nothing, just nothing. No bees disrupt the low sunbeams. Nothing makes any noise.

Even my howl is restricted to my insides, passing through my muscles but not exiting my body. This howl moves into my leg and I take a step, lifting my foot over the rock, the first step of many that will take me in the opposite direction of the city.

Here on the porch beside the muddy pond where five-legged frogs crawl over tumorous lily pads, someone dear to me asks why I always tell this story in the present tense. We lean back in our hand-hewn chairs, waving smoke sticks at the mosquitoes that churn around the slimy cattails. Soon it will be utterly dark in the abandoned swamp, no ambient light from anywhere, and we will retreat into the wooden cabin where the tilting floorboards remind us of the day we laid the clay foundation.

THE WEDDING STAIRS

At the tail end of the wedding, as the last guests were fight-ing over whose coat was whose, the maître d' took me aside. He'd had his eye on me all night; even when he'd handed me my third rosemary-cucumber martini in that dismissive way of his, still he'd had his eye on me.

I wondered, with some amazement, how he'd singled me out, my particular cocktail-length dress, my particular shoes; I was identical to every other drunk young lady at the wedding, in no way deserving of additional admiration or scorn, distinguished only by the fact that I happened to be the sole witness when the cancerous woman ran into the Ladies' Room with a nosebleed ("Can I get you seltzer perhaps?" I said, because the blood was falling on her green silk jacket and I've heard seltzer can do some good against blood. "It's my pancreas is all," she replied; I couldn't think of anything to say to that).

"I have to show you something," the maître d' said. They were the first words I'd heard from him, and while I wasn't surprised that his tone was scornful, I was surprised that he would make such a forthcoming statement.

We were standing at the bottom of a staircase, one of those staircases with red carpeting running down the middle; it was up this staircase that he gestured.

He was skinny, this maître d' of mine, almost skeletal, with a shorn head. His eyes were black and filled with rage or something else that made them burn. It was not hard to imagine him surviving a concentration camp.

In the dimness beyond the dance floor, my husband was leaned up against the wall, passed out there with a portrait of a woman from 1632 around his neck. I don't know how it had gotten there, that painting, but at the beginning of the evening it had been hanging grandly on the wall and now here it was with my husband's drunken head stuck through it, violating the lady's charcoal dress. I didn't know how much it would cost, or if our lives were essentially over.

"Of course," I said to the maître d', stepping onto the first stair.

Behind us, the bride and groom held each other weeping—hopefully for joy—in the starlight.

Just kidding. There was no starlight. In fact, the fluorescents had just come on; the staff was dying for us to clear out. But they *were* holding each other, the bride and the groom, and they were most definitely weeping. *With this ring, you are holy to me.*

The maître d' joined me on the step. I looked over at him, turning on the faucet of my smile, eager to dazzle him, to grab his hand and run upward. But yet again I'd misread the situation; he returned my gushing smile with that withering gaze of his, and my hand dangled un-held between us.

At a pace exactly halfway between slow and fast, the maître d' mounted the stairs, and I followed. There was a sharp right, then a second staircase. Hours we'd been here, in this old stone venue, hours of revelry, and I'd never had any idea about these staircases. What had happened to them, all my powers of observation? Already it was fading behind me, the wedding vanishing into the past, the things I shouldn't have said at all, much less in the middle of the dance floor: that my husband had desires I wasn't capable of satisfying, that my grief about the fetus had yet to drain away, that I wanted things to be different than the way they were.

I shivered with shame for that girl, that girl who had said those things, who had sat alone at an abandoned table trying to devour the dessert placed at her seat as well as the one at her husband's while the waiters looked on with distaste, but walking up these red-carpeted stairs alongside my maître d', I no longer felt responsible for the words I'd shed like dead hair upon the dance floor.

On the third staircase, the food began. At first, just a nibbled dinner roll in the corner of one stair. A whoosh of specks that might have been stains, or poppy seeds. A patch of something wet on the carpet—wine, or water, or an illusion.

But by the fourth staircase there was no question: the steps were littered with food. An unmistakable smear of that green pistachio mousse. A sprig of butter-encrusted sage. Gnocchi scattered moistly down the side.

With each step it got worse. The decimated body of a trout. A half-eaten fist of beef Wellington. A quail pulled to pieces. A slick of port sauce. The breathtaking garnishes—the rosemary, the begonias, the curls of candied lemon peel. The aftermath of the luxury, all just garbage now. Worse than garbage.

Then, on the sixth staircase, I got this odd feeling in my heart: there, unmistakable, were the remainders of the two desserts I'd failed to finish, the lavender crème brûlée still in its little cup, the hazelnut tart whose integrity I had violated.

Too ashamed to look at the maître d', I ducked my head and cried quietly as we passed the wasted desserts.

How fragrant these foods had been when they were bestowed upon the cream-colored tablecloths—the smell of butter, warmth, safety, joy. Yet now dark and disconcerting odors arose from the rejected food, the rot already encroaching. I had never before understood that the end of a feast is a funeral.

I didn't want to step on any of it—it seemed like stepping on corpses—but sometimes it was impossible to avoid, the food thicker on each stair. I shuddered as my shoe crushed an errant slice of blood orange, a handful of capers.

"You're right to feel pity," the maître d' said coldly on the ninth or maybe the tenth or maybe the nineteenth staircase, "but you're not supposed to direct that pity toward yourself."

It was impossible that this stone house contained all these staircases. We'd long ago shed the loveliness of the rooms below—the candlelight, the delicate white poppies, the old Dutch paintings. Here the red carpet looked cheap and stank. Bare bulbs, unfinished walls. We arrived at a paint-splattered plywood door.

The key that the maître d' removed from his inner pocket looked like a key from a fairy tale. Think Bluebeard; seven dead brides. Why did it take me so many staircases to realize the kind of danger I was in?

I whirled around to dash downward, but the maître d' somehow had his arm about my waist—what a long arm he had, a miraculous arm. I whirled back around to face him, hoping against hope that what he'd brought me here for was a kiss, but it only took one look at his mouth to know this was a cage, not an embrace. With his other hand he twisted the key.

Rows of washing machines. Rows and rows of washing machines. Brights and whites swirling, the gushing bubbles and water.

That was all. An enormous laundry room.

When I looked over at the maître d', I saw that he was smiling for the first time that night, and perhaps for the first time ever.

Strolling among the machines, in various states of undress (a shirt unbuttoned, a vest slung over a shoulder): waiters whose hairstyles I recognized from the banquet. Their faces, which had been blank blurs to me before, now seemed exceptionally vivid: an exhausted forehead, a wan smile, a cynical eyebrow.

"This," the maître d' told me, "is where we wash the costumes."

I wanted to ask him which costumes he meant, or if he'd misspoken, if he'd intended to say "the uniforms" or "the linens." But he was not the type to stand corrected.

Amid the aroma of laundry detergent, I caught a whiff of something less pleasant. I glanced down at myself, only to discover the gray fabric of my dress covered in old food, chunks of the feast plastered to the soles of my faux-vintage high heels, a layer of inexplicable stickiness on my skin; the odor emanated from me. I reached up to touch my hair—sure enough, smears of butter met my fingertips.

I hadn't worn a gray dress to the wedding! Yet I found myself unable to recall the original color of my dress—hadn't it been pink, or at least lavender? As I examined the dress, it struck me darkly that I recognized many of the stains now adorning it, recognized them by their shape and location; the red wine my husband spilled on my bodice at our own wedding, the sweat marks from the interview for the job I didn't get, semen and saliva, a teaspoon or two of amniotic fluid, the olive oil from the first dinner I'd ever cooked by myself, the requisite menstrual blotch, the mud from the hill behind my grandmother's house, the grass stains from where I'd sat on the lawn as a baby. And brownish droplets on my sleeve, which I could only attribute to the cancerous woman with the bloody nose.

"Excuse me," I said to the maître d', hesitant yet also desperate, desperate. "Can we wash my—costume?"

The word "costume" felt awkward in my mouth—"dress" was the word I'd have preferred.

I pictured myself unzipping my dress, unhooking my bra, stepping out of my shoes and underwear, standing there in the laundry room among the waitstaff, heavy-limbed and calm, like a child who's never heard of sex. Maybe they would gather around me, poke at me or mock me or tickle me, or maybe the vast indifference they currently exhibited would continue. It didn't matter, though; nothing mattered as long as my costume got washed.

"You don't want that," the maître d' said simply, as though he already knew that in two days' time I'd bust my knee while stomping my foot on the sidewalk during a fight with my husband, already knew that soon my husband would cup my face in his hands and truthfully say, "When I am an old man, I will look back on this as the happiest time of my life," already knew that I'd truthfully reply, "When I am an old woman, I will look back on this as the happiest time of my life," already knew that for years and years we'd alternate between the foot-stomping and the face-cupping, that I'd limp down the cereal aisle on my busted knee, that my heart would lift with joy in the produce section, that I'd wince among the pastas and laugh past the milk, back and forth, again and again, on and on, forever, until the day I once more entered the laundry room.

CONTAMINATION GENERATION

Our daughter knows the word "lawn," of course she does, and the word still sounds green, it still sounds like leisure. And there are still people, rich people, like the Stanhopes on the other side of the wall, who have private lawns.

But when we take Lulu for a very special fifth birthday outing to the Botanical Gardens across the city (bus, subway, bus, grass for the masses) and promenade the lawn where the cherry trees are blossoming, she asks, "What's all this grass for?," and then I feel bad, like why the heck didn't we bring her here when she turned two, three, four?

And then I'm remembering that time last summer when we rode the subway out to the shore and I said, "Don't you love the sound of the sea?" and she said, "Yeah, just like Wave-Maker!," which is the machine we've used ever since she was born to try to drown out the sound of sirens and other bad things. And then I'm remembering when we took her to the urban stables, five-minute pony rides on the sidewalk for sixteen dollars a pop every Sunday morning, the dirty white pony ("Marshmallow") stepping carefully among blowing candy wrappers, and though Lulu was so stiff with terror that I had to pull her off after forty-five seconds, she insisted I feed Marshmallow a few of the baby carrots we'd brought along.

The truth is we hadn't taken her to the Botanical Gardens when she turned two, three, four, because we'd taken her there when she turned one. We'd set her down on the lawn, so pleased with ourselves, all ready to snap a bunch of photos, but she'd burst into tears—she was scared of the grass, she kept jerking her hands up as though the grass was burning her, she looked at us like, *Hey, what's wrong with the floor?*

Lulu, five years old now, staring at the lawn at the Botanical Gardens. Lulu. A spritely, springy name. A name for feeling carefree. But our Lulu is serious. The friendly cashiers always say, "Those *eyes!*" but I can hear the note of fear. I get it. The largeness of her eyes. The darkness. My dark little thin little odd little glittering shadow child. I put my hand on her disproportionately large head, 90th percentile. Big brain, we told her when a kid on the playground said something a couple weeks back.

"It's a lawn," I explain. "For playing." My throat surprises itself by clogging up. In the city parks, the streambeds are empty except for old soda cans, used condoms, dirty napkins, plastic bags, cigarette butts, rabies vaccination pellets. Back where I grew up, or I guess more accurately, back *when* I grew up, I was king of a creek.

"No," Lulu corrects, pointing at a wooden sign: NO PLAYING ON THE GRASS.

Sarah gives that cold laugh of hers. "Kid's right," she says. Don't get me wrong, Sarah is the best, my great big love, but she didn't grow up anywhere where she could be king of a creek and sometimes that makes her less kind than, say, me.

"It's for *looking*," I correct myself. "For en*joy*ing. For feeling the *green* in your eyes. The green in your bean."

"The green in your dream," Lulu plays.

"That's my girl," I say like a dad in a movie. I shoot a look at Sarah. Sarah smiles back at me. So nice. A family on a lawn, or *near* a lawn, at the Botanical Gardens on this fine day, half a decade into the life of Lulu, into the life of Sarah and Danny as parents.

"Well," I say, "maybe you can't play on it, but you can walk on it. Go ahead, Lu. Walk on the grass. Walk on it. It'll feel nice." I push her gently forward.

Lulu pauses at the boundary between the paved path and the grass. She dips her foot in its jelly sandal onto the grass as though the grass is a body of water with a dangerous current.

"It tickles," she whispers.

"It's nice, right?" I encourage. "It's nice. Go ahead. Walk on it."

I place my own foot on the lawn, the prickles of grass poking up between the holes in my sandals. In a sudden fit of exuberance, I throw myself down. Until this moment, I hadn't realized that Lulu is old enough to find me embarrassing. I can see the love and the embarrassment fighting on her face as she watches me. But there's no one nearby, and I decide to go all the way. I fling my legs out and lie star-shaped on the grass.

"Yodeleheho!" I say.

"Danny," Sarah says. She too is half-ashamed, half-admiring the way I am. The joy I can contain. She points at a second wooden sign: NO WALKING, SITTING, OR LYING ON THE GRASS.

"There's a guy coming," Lulu says.

"Hello, guy," I say unconcernedly. But I stand up, hoping I've gotten at least a couple of grass stains on my khaki shorts.

The Botanical Gardens employee changes course.

"Does this remind you of anything?" I ask Lulu, gesturing wide to encompass the rolling lawn, the trees and trellises, the prettiest place I have to offer her. I'm thinking of a print book we like to read together, an old textbook called *Flora*.

Lulu follows the sweep of my arm as it directs her gaze toward more green than she ever gets to see in one place.

She grabs my other arm and looks up at me soberly, hopefully, aiming to please.

"It reminds me of money," she says.

I don't know if Lulu meant money because money is green, is the sort of green she sees more often than the other sort of green, or if she already understands that rich people have lawns whereas people like us don't whereas some people don't have produce or computers or homes. I didn't want to probe, back there at the Botanical Gardens, but my mood did a nosedive, that's for sure, a nosedive that's landed me in the concrete enclosure behind our apartment building at ten o'clock at night, but I'm not out here to dump trash or recycling, I'm just checking on the moon, orange through layers of smog. The moon never looked this awesome when I was a kid. I stand there looking at it, challenging myself to ignore the smell of over-warm trash, until the moon scoots a couple inches and gets obscured by the wall.

On the other side of the wall, where the moon is still visible, the Stanhopes are splashing in their pool. I can hear it, alongside the noise of their generator, humming as it always hums, purifying the air on their lawn, incinerating the mosquitoes.

How do I know all this about the Stanhopes' lawn? Well, there's a hole, believe it or not, a tiny peephole at the place where the Stanhopes' amalgamated quartz and rubber wall meets the side of our concrete enclosure, a fact that came to my attention some months ago, a fact that I haven't shared with Lulu or Sarah because what good would it do them to see this. It is a wrong thing, one of the wrong things, how near to each other the rich and the not-rich live. Steve Stanhope is an inventor, or not an inventor, an investor in inventors—he finds the scientists who are doing the cool things and figures out how to get them to the people. I think you have to admire that.

"Daddy! Daddy!" the sons (twins) cry out as Steve Stanhope throws them again and again into the pool. I scoff at the irresponsible parenting—who lets their kids stay up this late?

Sure, Lulu's bedroom might be a cubbyhole carved out of our bedroom with a temporary wall, and sure, maybe I was a little wounded when Lulu proudly led a new friend into her room and the girl said, "Why is your room so dark and small?," but at least we put her to bed at a healthy hour, and read her print books beforehand, and give her a little bit of the special organic kids' toothpaste, arm and a leg but worth it, god, well worth it, for her. And now I'm remembering the time a few weeks back when I happened to peek through the wall during the twins' birthday party, and who should I see there but Marshmallow—looking maybe a little bit cleaner, sure, but skinny old Marshmallow nonetheless, marching wearily up and down that lawn just as he'd marched up and down the sidewalk for Lulu.

Right as I'm trying to get myself onto my high horse about what great parents Sarah and I are, Mara Stanhope steps out onto the patio in these soft gray harem pants, and I realize with a start that she's pregnant, pregnant as a pumpkin but still somehow so lean, standing in the light of her double glass doors.

Three children. Imagine that. It was already a luxury to have two. Even if we could somehow get the money together again for the fertility treatments (which no way could we), no way could we afford a second. It had taken Sarah two years to conceive. "Plastics," the doctors explained. So you go home and it's like, the yogurt's in plastic, the shampoo's in plastic, the toothbrushes are plastic.

Mara Stanhope bore the twins surrounded by a pod of dolphins at sunset in the ocean off a black volcanic sand beach in Hawaii. The pics were gorgeous, and public, on the Internet, with her privates blocked out. *DOLPHIN-ASSISTED CHILDBIRTH SUCCESS! DOLPHIN MIDWIFERY LEADS TO DREAM BIRTH!* "It's about coexistence," Mara Stanhope was quoted as saying. "It's about total relaxation."

"Boys!" she says now, resting a hand on her pert belly. "Aiden! Landon! Bedtime!"

When Sarah was pregnant she would always say, "I'm starving for something but I have no idea what it is." One night I spy Mara Stanhope lounging on the torch-lit lawn with a tray of small bowls, eating a bit from this or that with a tiny fork, but I can tell she's just like Sarah was, starving for something that hasn't yet been tasted by anyone on this planet. She reaches into the stainless-steel cooler, then settles back into her lounge chair with plain old Coca-Cola in a can.

"Hey witness," Sarah says, coming up behind me.

I startle. It's nearly midnight—Lulu has been in bed for hours, and so has Sarah. She's wearing her great little blue robe.

"There's a peephole here," I say stupidly.

"I know." Sarah smiles in the slight light. "Pretty fun, huh?"

I love my wife.

"She's had some wild cravings," she says. "All those capers."

Above us a spot of light moves across the purple clouds.

"Another fucking searchlight," she whispers. "Voulez-vous coucher avec moi ce soir?"

Sarah and I, we get sad about different things.

Like that night, later on, I think about how Lulu doesn't recognize stars except as a shape in coloring books and on stickers and stuff. I say that to Sarah. "Isn't that sad?" I say.

"No."

"It doesn't make you sad?"

"Everyone has lots to learn about everything."

When I get home from work that Friday, Lulu is sitting on Sarah's lap, helping her order the groceries. Lulu has outgrown this activity a bit, her legs splaying awkwardly over Sarah. I remember going to the grocery store with my mom, helping her choose the honeydew based on how hollow they sounded when you knocked on them.

"No, Mom!" she says to Sarah, both of them staring at the screen. "Rutabaga only gets two and a half stars this week."

"It's on sale, Lu," Sarah says. "A girl's gotta do what a girl's gotta do."

Lulu jumps off Sarah's lap and runs over to me.

"Daddy! Let's search for something!"

This is it: getting home from work on Friday, better than cool water.

"Sure thing. Hmm, how about . . ."

"The world's tiniest marsupial?"

"Sure thing," I say.

"Okay, but after dinner," Sarah says.

"Lemme guess," Lulu says. "Rutabaga?"

"You bet," Sarah says curtly.

After dinner Lulu and I search the Internet to find the world's tiniest marsupial.

"Don't touch," I say when she goes to press her fingertips against the close-up of the creature's fur. "You'll leave marks."

She pulls her hand away from the screen.

Sarah takes the trash out after Lulu goes to bed but she doesn't come back. After ten minutes I go to look for her. I find her in the concrete enclosure, face glued to the hole in the wall.

"Hey witness," I say, pushing her aside so I can see.

"Hey addict," she counters, pushing me back.

"Is that what I think it is?" Mara Stanhope's low moan stretches over the wall, over the noise of the generator.

"No, sicko," Sarah hisses. "You think I'd wanna watch *that*?"

I arrange myself above Sarah, like the next head up on a totem pole, so that we can peer through the hole at the same time.

In the light of many moon-shaped paper lanterns, Mara Stanhope is crouched naked on all fours, clinging to the thick grass of the lawn, rolling her hips around and around, emitting groans that swing back and forth between pleasure and pain. A slender woman in a gray shift pours golden oil onto her back and kneels to rub it in. A second slender woman in a gray shift crouches in front of Mara, also on all fours, groaning along with her.

"Those are the doulas," Sarah whispers. Sarah had wanted a doula (just one) for a hot second, until we learned how much they cost. *Not a biggie,* she'd said back then.

"I guess they got sick of the dolphins," I say, hoping Sarah hasn't noticed the rose petals floating in the pool.

I await her laugh but she ignores me.

"Wonder where *he* is," I say.

Whatever else you might say about Lulu's birth—that the nurses had cold and impatient hands, that the anesthesiologist didn't inspire confidence as he poked the needle yet again into Sarah's spine, that the doctor yawned seven times while stitching up Sarah's vagina—I was there, instant by instant, and as she pushed Lulu's head out I said to her, *I didn't think I could be in more awe of you than I already was.*

Music swells up from the Stanhopes' outdoor speakers, music that sounds like it was composed by the cosmos, and Steve Stanhope strides out of the glass door. Mara Stanhope's moans unite with the chords of the music, and he comes over to her, and the doulas tactfully move aside, and he gets down on all fours facing his wife, and he too moans the moans of the universe, and believe me, I wish it was a laughable sight but somehow it's not.

"You are now ten thousand times more relaxed than you've ever been," the doulas chant.

If only Sarah would laugh. Instead she mutters something.

"What?" I demand.

"The rich still get to be animals," she says.

Lulu emerged with the assistance of K-Y Jelly, but the Stanhopes' daughter is born into a rush of imported organic olive oil, the doulas pouring cupful after cupful of it to serve as lubrication, and as the baby's head emerges onto the candlelit lawn, Mara Stanhope seems to be having the deepest orgasm of her life, and I'm ashamed by my hardening, but more ashamed by the way Sarah waggles her butt against me to acknowledge the hardening, but mainly turned on by the idea of going inside with Sarah and filling her up with triplets.

Two people in medical coats race onto the lawn to collect the blood from the umbilical cord. Which, yes, will cost the Stanhopes 75 percent of our monthly income to store in a private blood bank.

"Please no," Sarah says when the doulas present to the Stanhopes the disk of the slimy, wound-up umbilical cord (*Once it dries out, it's the ideal chew toy for the baby!*).

By Saturday afternoon, Mara Stanhope is stretched out in her lounge chair beneath an umbrella. She looks like a woman at a spa, not a woman who gave birth less than twenty-four hours ago. That smell of newly cut grass. She's holding a tall glass containing a bloodred drink, sipping the liquid through a long straw.

"OMG," Sarah says after taking a peek. "A placenta smoothie. Let me take Lu to ballet today, okay? All these good vibes are killing me."

I saw Sarah's (or, I guess, Lulu's) placenta for about five seconds before it was tossed into a container of organs and wheeled away.

A nurse carries a woven basket out onto the lawn. It takes me a minute to realize that the baby is inside the basket. The nurse places the baby on Mara Stanhope's chest and Mara pulls her robe aside and the newborn takes the nipple easily, almost lazily, like an old pro. Those early days with Lulu, when she barely nursed, and then there was the heat wave, I prefer not to think about, Sarah hooked up to the breast pump for hours every day, me trying to pretend the pump didn't freak me out. "What's wrong?" Sarah sobbed, her nipples extending and retracting inside the plastic tubing. "Nothing, sorry, sorry," I kept saying, cradling Lulu.

The nurse leaves and Steve Stanhope comes out. He looks happy, healthy. He sits at the base of Mara's lounge chair, stroking her shin. They smile and talk quietly. I can't tell what they're saying, except that I keep hearing the word "lake," "lake," "lake," the syllable punctuating their every sentence.

He wanders off and she reclines, closes her eyes. Their vegetable garden is thriving already, even this early in the season. I can see the kale and mint from here.

"Excuse me," the voice says, or rather the mouth, the mouth right against my eye, breath in my pupil.

I leap back and cover my eye as though it's been burned.

"Pardon me," the mouth says. "I noticed this hole the other day. I'll have our guy seal it up ASAP."

Steve Stanhope speaks graciously, maybe even with compassion, as though he knows it isn't good for me or anyone else in my building to witness the activity on his lawn.

"Oh, no problem," I say, annoyed with myself for how grateful I feel that he's playing it as though he's inconvenienced me rather than the reverse.

Then it's his eye at the hole. His eye upon the deteriorating brick, the row of trash cans swollen with garbage, Lulu's hand-me-down scooter chained to the communal bike rack. The eye lingers.

"Hey, screw you!" I say.

The eye doesn't react. Had I whispered it too softly for him to hear? Had I said it at all?

"Say, neighbor," Steve Stanhope says. "My wife gave birth to a baby girl last night, and I'd love to give you a little something as a kind of celebratory gift, because, well, there's nothing like having a baby girl."

As if I don't know.

"Sort of like the way I'd've given you a cigar back in the day, you know?"

"Okay," I say.

"Just a sec," he says. And even though I don't want anything from Steve Stanhope, I stay there at the peephole, waiting. Maybe if he hadn't said "Say," I might not have stayed. But it's a tic of mine too sometimes, to say "Say."

I'm keeping an eye on the peephole when suddenly I sense a flutter at the top of my head, like a bird just pooped on my hair. I look up to find the tiniest drone I've ever seen hovering above me. The drone beeps and drops something small onto the concrete beside me.

"Hey, pick it up," Steve Stanhope requests. I bend down to retrieve the object. It's a perfectly round pebble, pure white, like the moon of my boyhood. "You can plant it between the cracks in concrete. It'll grow wherever."

"Ste-eve!" Mara sings out across the lawn. "Ste-eve!"

"Gotta run." The eye winks. "Enjoy, okay? Nice chatting

with you. And don't worry, the hole will be repaired any day now."

"Does it need water?" I remember to ask only once he's out of earshot.

"You can do it!" I say to Lulu. Dusk on Saturday, and we're standing above the seam between two slabs of concrete in the enclosure behind the building. Sarah refused to come outside.

"A weird random magic pebble seed thingy?" Sarah had said, scrubbing hard at the nonorganic apples in the sink. "From Steve *Stanhope*? No thanks."

"It's a gift," I countered. "From a neighbor."

"Isn't he the one who put those radioactive fish in the canal to eat the other even more radioactive fish?"

"I don't know what you're talking about," I lied.

"Well don't let Lulu touch it," she said.

Now, as we stand at the back of the building, I drop the seed into Lulu's palm.

"It's cold!" she gasps.

"Looks like the moon, right?" I say. "I mean, that's what the moon used to look like."

"Okay," she says.

Okay.

"So," I say. "Plant it."

"Where?" She looks around the concrete enclosure. "Is there some dirt?"

"Well actually," I explain, "this is a special kind of seed. It doesn't need even the teensiest bit of dirt."

"Okay," she says again. Sometimes I worry about Lulu.

She doesn't seem like a child at all. She never uses words like "teensiest."

"So all you have to do is just plant it right here between these pieces of concrete. See?" I stroke the seam with the tip of my sneaker. I've never seen anything green in our backyard, not even weeds poking up between the cracks.

"So, I should plant it?" she says. "Like, put it here?"

Carefully, she places the seed on the seam.

"Well," I say, trying to pull my mood up by my own bootstraps, "is that where you want your plant to grow? You have to think these things through."

"Well," Lulu says, "I guess someone might step on it when they were taking their trash out. So maybe we should—put it somewhere else?"

I get the distinct feeling that she's humoring me. Lulu is so good at love. I'm the oldest in our household, followed by Sarah and then Lulu. But in terms of souls, Lulu's the oldest and I'm the youngest.

"*Plant* it somewhere else," I correct her.

"Yeah," she says.

"You decide." I pluck the seed off the ground and place it in her palm again.

She walks around the concrete enclosure, cupping the seed, examining all the seams. It takes her about forty-five seconds. We're talking six feet by ten feet, max. A siren wails by on the street and—absentmindedly, accurately, the way I used to hum along when a familiar song came on the radio—Lulu imitates its howl under her breath.

Then she stops and plants the seed between two slabs. By

"plants" I mean she shoves the pebble as far as it can be shoved into the crack.

On the other side of the wall, the Stanhopes' generator hums maddeningly. I wonder if we reap any benefit from living so near it.

"Fun, huh?" I say as she stands up. I'm expecting her to be polite and accommodating when she glances at me, enthusiastic for my sake.

But there's an actual glow in her eyes, the delight moving slow and stately across her face.

She says, "I should water it, right?"

Bingo.

"No," Sarah whispers. I'm holding her, spooning her from behind on the bed. Tomorrow will be Monday. "It's not right. I just think—I just think kids now. I mean, our kids. The kids of people like us. They face—they face a lot of—they don't have—the world—the schools—a lot of disappointment, you know? On a daily basis, right? Like, I heard of a boy who got a ticket for drawing a chalk dragon on the sidewalk. Her school doesn't own a single microscope, okay? So I just don't think—"

"It's too late," I whisper back. "She planted the seed. She watered the seed."

"It's not a seed," Sarah hisses.

"Be that as it may," I say serenely.

" 'Be that as it may'!" Sarah whisper-yells. "Are you stupid? Seriously, sometimes I seriously think you are stupid."

"She can hear us maybe, you know," I say. Because if Lulu is awake, which hopefully she isn't, but if she is, she can hear us even over WaveMaker. That's how thin the walls are.

On Tuesday evening, the temperature is forty-five degrees higher when I leave my office building than when I entered it in the morning.

"Feels like end times, huh?" a janitor says, laughing as I pass him on my way out to the street.

"Sure thing," I say to be nice, but then my words stick with me all the way down into the subway. *Sure thing sure thing sure thing sure thing.*

"Where's Lulu?" I ask Sarah the second I step through the door. It had been a long bad day. I'd spent nine hours feeling like my computer was an eye disapproving of my every action.

"Out back," Sarah replies, scrubbing rutabaga in the sink. I can feel her blaming me.

I throw my bag down and run out the door.

There she is, staring at the crack in the concrete. She looks up at me and the day falls away from my shoulders.

"Hey kiddo," I say.

"It disappeared!" she announces like it's good news.

So the seed is gone. So a rabid squirrel squirreled it away, or the super finally got around to sweeping up.

"I can't see it anymore!" Lulu says. "It must've sunk down to put in its roots!"

I've always thought Lulu is more like Sarah in temperament. Darker, tending toward pessimism. But now it occurs to me (with horror) that maybe Lulu is more like me. Relentlessly optimistic.

"Well well well," I say, far more accustomed to Lulu's solemnity than to her glee. "How about that. Let's go in and have some dinner, okay?"

"Aren't you glad, Daddy?" she says.

"Oh," I say, feeling sad. "I am so glad."

"Thank you for the seed." Lulu gazes down at the crack in the concrete. "I gave it a few more drops of water. Is that okay?"

She's wearing her blue school uniform. The humidity frizzes her hair and shines her skin. Sometimes she looks so wonderful I have to shut my eyes.

I say, "Let's go see what Mom came up with for dinner."

Inside, Sarah has set the table with cloth napkins. She's lit a candle. Sarah is the kind of person who can create something out of nothing, a skill that's coming in more and more handy. Cleverly, she sautés rutabaga leaves with garlic. She roasts the flesh with oil and Italian seasoning and calls it rutabaga gnocchi, and sure, the chunks of it are not entirely unlike gnocchi.

I have this trick where I flick my fingers against the side of my taut cheek to make a sound like a drop of water falling into a body of water. It's a refreshing sound, and Lulu loves it. Given the hotness of the night, I make the drop-of-water sound a bunch of times as we sit down to dinner.

Lulu claps. Sarah rolls her eyes.

"Ugh, stop it," she says. "That sound depresses me."

"Why?" Lulu demands.

"Reminds me of the drought."

"Well it reminds me of the rain!" Lulu says.

Parenthood is underrated, because there's no way to talk about it. How can these chemicals and minerals, the chemicals and minerals of Lulu, add up to this?

We try to be good parents. We try to foster compassion, independence, thriftiness. We permit Lulu to go by herself down the street to the bodega. We give her an allowance if she makes her bed every day. We let her hang out with Mason Mitchell, the unpleasant boy on the third floor whose parents don't care if he plays video games all day and whose home doesn't contain a single print book. We try to not freak out when Mason's mother gives them Mountain Dew for dinner. A kid needs friends, especially an only child.

But sometimes I don't think we're doing it right. It feels, at times, impossible. I've come upon Lulu browsing the Internet, staring silently at pictures of starving children and people drowned in tsunamis. I've watched her watch a video billboard screening a liquor ad in which seven almost naked women dance around a man in a tuxedo.

Sarah is strong but sometimes at night she's been known to weep. *We're all she has, and we're not enough.*

Yet on Thursday evening, when Lulu meets me at the front door of the apartment building, jumping up and down, grabbing my hand, yanking me along toward the back door, it feels like we are doing something right.

Bless Steve Stanhope. Because there's a half-centimeter chunk of glittery white matter emerging from the crack in the concrete. Before I can bend down to examine it more closely, Lulu flings herself into my arms as she hasn't since she was a toddler. That's the thing, you hold your kids less and less with each passing day until one day you hardly get to touch them at all.

Sarah refuses to come outside and look at the growing thing. She barely glances at our glowing faces.

"I'm sure it's great," she says.

I head to the kitchen for a glass of cold water. I like to drink cold water when I'm annoyed. Put out the fire. My hand is on the tap when Sarah calls from the other room, "Contaminated!"

"What?" I snap.

"They put out the announcement an hour ago."

I grunt in her direction, as though it's her fault.

"Only for forty-eight hours. There's a gallon of bottled in the fridge. We can boil more too."

"But it's so hot in here already," I say.

Lulu and Sarah are silent in the other room.

"Thank you," I say, ashamed of myself, and open the fridge.

The night turns out just great, though. We have rutabaga with brown sugar and allspice for dessert. Lulu and I go out to check on the growing thing after dinner and it's still there, a small sparkle in the dark. The Stanhopes' generator purrs away on the other side of the wall. And though I can hear the twins splashing in the pool, the moist noise seeping through the peephole, Lulu doesn't seem to notice—she's never been in a pool, so maybe the sound doesn't even register. We come back inside and boil a bunch of water and hang out and read print books and Lulu falls asleep smiling.

Then we turn on WaveMaker, and the apartment takes on that special hush, and Sarah pulls out the CockFrolick and steps out of her work dress and skin is still skin, you know?

"No respite," Sarah says at two in the morning.

What's driving her crazy is the noise from the upstairs neighbors, who stream violent movies all night long.

I get up and go into the bathroom and buy a campfire app. I return to bed, a fire flickering on the screen of my phone, the sound of crickets and crackling sap joining the Wave-Maker in the battle against the sound effects. I place the phone beside her on the pillow and swipe the volume up to its maximum level. The audio is fantastic. I can practically smell the wood smoke.

"Turn that off," Sarah says.

"It's working!"

"No," she says.

When I listen hard, I can still hear the movie raging upstairs, and maybe it's almost worse, listening for that beneath the sound of the campfire. But I don't pause the app.

"Please," she says. "Seriously, it sucks. Don't you think it sucks?"

"I think it's good," I say.

"That's depressing," she says, rolling away from me.

I pause the app. I consider and reject the possibility of proposing a nighttime stroll. We do that sometimes, when we both can't sleep, use Google maps to take a walk on a Greek isle or through a Peruvian village. We hold hands while one of us scrolls.

Sarah rolls back toward me, apologetic.

"You know what I hate?" she says. "Those screen savers at work that show one gorgeous nature scene after another."

A siren down the block launches its long wail. We lie there listening.

"Remember Lulu dancing naked in front of the mirror when she was two, wearing all your necklaces?" I say.

Sarah stiffens, surprised out of her crankiness.

"She's experienced plenty of joy," I say.

Our heads are so close together that I can feel her nodding.

"There's something I haven't told you," Sarah says.

I get nervous.

"Sometimes when you take the recycling out and I hear you through the window clanging the metal bucket against the container," she says, "it sounds like the opening drumbeat of this awesome and never-before-played rock song."

By the time I get home from work on Friday, Lulu's plant is a quarter of an inch tall, a glittering globular dime-sized cluster oozing out of the concrete. She crouches down to drip a few drops of pre-boiled water on it. The contamination warning has been extended through the weekend.

"I'm sure contaminated water is just fine for *it*," Sarah said, sweating in the kitchen, where now there's always water boiling on the stove.

But Lulu insisted.

"Do you love my crystal plant?" Lulu asks, looking up at me.

I steal another quick glance over her shoulder. The thing glints in the dusk. This is a good one, Steve Stanhope. Flowers for city kids. Magic for the contamination generation. Thank you, sir.

I've never seen Lulu this happy. Being happy, that's how you thank your parents. That's all you have to do.

All evening Lulu and I are like two mirrors, reflecting excitement back and forth at each other. She strokes my arm while I read *Flora* to her. Together we do an Internet search about cacti.

"You two," Sarah says.

After Lulu goes to sleep, I head out back to examine the crystal plant in the orange moonlight. But en route I get waylaid by shouting coming from the Stanhopes' lawn. I shouldn't rush over to the peephole. I rush over to the peephole.

It's been covered over. Thank goodness. Who wants to see that damn lawn anyway.

Well, me.

I put my ear up to the place where the hole used to be. In the great distance, Steve Stanhope is yelling a one-sided fight, presumably into a cell phone. "Beta? Beta!"

"What's eating you?" Sarah says back inside.

"You should go and check out that thing back there," I say. "Pretty cool stuff."

Early Saturday morning, before Sarah and Lulu are up, I'm taking out the recycling yet again (I don't know how three people can create so much waste), and there, in the bald humid light of day, I see the crystal plant for what it is.

I drop the recycling bucket and kneel down.

Five or so pebbles, rolled in glue and then glitter, stacked messily atop each other, drizzled with more glue, more glitter. The same old school glue they sell at the bodega. The glitter from tubes.

I am stupid.

I go back inside, shutting the door against the grind of the Stanhopes' generator.

Sarah is sitting at the table with a cup of instant coffee. We switched to instant after they doubled the tax on imports. I'm touched by the sight of her.

"Thanks for doing that," I say, ashamed. "It's not totally convincing, but thank you."

"Hm?" she says absently. She's reading the news on her small screen. For her this is as good as it gets. Saturday morning, silence, coffee, screen.

"The 'plant.' That you made. For Lulu."

"UN Considers Proposal to Construct International Landfills in North Pole," she reads. "Is that good or bad?"

I open Lulu's flimsy door and step into her room. I turn off the WaveMachine. She's sleeping on her back, her arms flung above her head as they were whenever she slept as a baby. Her breathing sounds as good to me as water running in a creek.

Before I slide open the drawer beneath her bed, I already know what I will find hidden in the back corner: the glue, the glitter.

When Lulu was newborn we called her Muskrat, though neither of us really knows what a muskrat is. It was just that she seemed like a small, mysterious mammal. I remember the way she would arch her tiny eyebrows when I picked her up after she'd finished drinking as much as she could get from Sarah's nipple. I'd hold her under her arms, in constant fear of dislocating them from her little shoulder sockets, and she'd raise those eyebrows, halfway a queen disapproving of something, halfway an animal startled out of its nest in its moment of deepest respite. I have no photograph of this face Lulu used to make, it was far too fleeting to ever catch, but that face of hers, those eyebrows peaked, imperious, disoriented, that is the face of my life.

How many times did I call Sarah from work to ask, "Is she still breathing?"

I don't touch the glue or the glitter. Lulu is awake now. I can feel it, can feel her pretending she's still asleep. I shut the drawer and leave the room and (what's this giddiness I feel?) wait for Lulu to come out, whenever she's ready. The thing is, the organism survives no matter what; the organism even thrives.

ACKNOWLEDGMENTS

This book was written over the course of the past decade. In that time, I have been beyond fortunate to receive a great deal of nurturing and support from a great many individuals and institutions. It is a profound delight to acknowledge:

My agent, Faye Bender, for her tranquillity and her guidance.

My editor, Sarah Bowlin, with whom it has been a joy to collaborate, and the rest of the Henry Holt team, especially Leslie Brandon, Kerry Cullen, Lucy Kim, Jason Liebman, and Maggie Richards.

The editors who assisted me in revising drafts of these stories, especially Halimah Marcus, Benjamin Samuel, and Rob Spillman.

The publications in which pieces from this book first appeared, some in slightly different form: "The Knowers" in *Electric Literature*; "The Messy Joy of the Final Throes of the Dinner Party" on PRI's *Selected Shorts*; "Life Care Center" in *The Iowa Review*; "The Joined" in *Mississippi Review*; "Flesh and Blood" and "Children" in *Tin House*; "When the Tsunami Came" in *The Pinch*; "One of Us Will Be Happy; It's Just a Matter of Which One" in *Fairy Tale Review*; "Things We Do" in *DIAGRAM*; "R" and "How I Began to Bleed Again After Six Alarming Months Without" in *Unstuck*; "The Worst" in *ArtFaccia*; "The Beekeeper" in *Isthmus*; and "Wedding Stairs" in *Slice.*

The Rona Jaffe Foundation, the Whiting Foundation, the Ucross Foundation, and Symphony Space.

Lisa Graziano of Leapfrog Press, for publishing my first book, and Krista Marino of Delacorte, for publishing my second.

My teachers and colleagues, current and former, in the Brooklyn College Department of English, including Julie Agoos, L. A. Asekoff, Elaine Brooks, Erin Courtney, Michael Cunningham, James Davis, Joshua Henkin, Janet Moser, and Elissa Schappell, with infinite thanks to Jenny Offill, Ellen Tremper, and Mac Wellman.

My former classmates in the Brooklyn College MFA program, especially Jeanie Gosline, Andy Hunter, Reese Kwon, Scott Lindenbaum, Elissa Matsueda, Joseph Rogers, and Margaret Zamos-Monteith.

The searingly insightful members, current and former, of the Imitative Fallacies, including Adam Brown, David Ellis, Tom Grattan, Anne Ray, and Mohan Sikka, with special thanks to Marie-Helene Bertino, Elizabeth Logan Harris, Elliott Holt, and Amelia Kahaney.

My students, who have graced my classrooms and my life with their curiosity and intelligence.

My dear friends Sarah Baron, Sarah Brown, Adam Farbiarz, Aysu Farbiarz, David Gorin, Lucas Hanft, Avni Jariwala, Jeremy Kahan, Debra Morris, Jonas Oransky, Laura Perciasepe, Genevieve Randa, Kendyl Salcito, Maisie Tivnan, and Tess Wheelwright, with extra thanks to Andy Vernon-Jones for the photographs.

My wonderful family: my parents, Paul Phillips and Susan Zimmermann; my grandparents Paul Phillips Sr. and Mary Jane Zimmermann; my in-laws, Gail and Doug Thompson; my siblings-in-law, Peter Light, Raven Phillips, and Nate Thompson; my brother, Mark Phillips; my sister Katherine Phillips (you are still at my side); and my two dreamy little nieces. My sister Alice Light is the best adviser imaginable, in matters of both literature and life.

My children, Ruth and Neal, "a detonation in my heart." You're where the fun is.

Adam: Thank you for the past thirteen years. You know why this book is for you.

About the Author

Helen Phillips is the recipient of a Rona Jaffe Foundation Writer's Award and the Italo Calvino Prize, among others. She is the author of the widely acclaimed novel *The Beautiful Bureaucrat* (a *New York Times* Notable Book) and the collection *And Yet They Were Happy* (named a notable book by the Story Prize). Her work has appeared on *Selected Shorts* and in *Tin House, Electric Literature,* and *The New York Times.* An assistant professor of creative writing at Brooklyn College, she lives in Brooklyn with her husband and children.

Milton Keynes UK
Ingram Content Group UK Ltd.
UKHW041320301024
2472UKWH00040B/353